Dogwood Stew
and Catnip Tea

Dogwood Stew and Catnip Tea

A Granny Green-Gloves
Adventure

JEAN STEPHENSON

CROSSWAY BOOKS • WHEATON, ILLINOIS
A DIVISION OF GOOD NEWS PUBLISHERS

Special thanks to Bill and Audrey Reed
whose hospitality was incredibly generous
and whose quest for the Pink Farm
was one I'll never forget.

Dogwood Stew and Catnip Tea.

Copyright © 1993 by Jean Stephenson.

Published by Crossway Books, a division of Good News Publishers,
1300 Crescent St., Wheaton, Illinois 60187.

Cover illustration: Wayne Hovis

Art Direction/Design: Mark Schramm

First printing, 1993

Printed in the United States of America

Library of Congress Cataloging-in-Publication Data
Stephenson, Jean.
    Dogwood stew and catnip tea / Jean Stephenson.
        p.   cm.
    Summary: Angry at having to share her bedroom for the summer
with her loud and unconventional grandmother, eleven-year-old Annika
has her view of the world changed by her grandmother's knowledge of
life and Jesus.
    [1. Grandmothers—Fiction.   2. Christian life—Fiction.]
I. Title.
PZ7.S83654Do 1993   [Fic]—dc20   92-40804
ISBN 0-89107-717-0

01		00		99		98		97		96		95		94		93
15	14	13	12	11	10	9	8	7	6	5	4	3	2	1

*To the memory of
Gran*

*and to
Drew, Austin, Annika,
John Mark and Chase,
who never knew her;
may you all know her
faith and her joy.*

Granny
Green-Gloves

Dear Annika,

In three weeks' time, I will be getting on the airplane in Nashville and coming to stay with you in Washington. I understand you're giving up your room for me, and I want you to know how greatly I appreciate this sacrifice on your part. You are such a sweet girl to do this for your grandmother. Your mamma and daddy seem to think it's a good idea that I come stay with you all awhile now that I'm alone. We'll see how things go this summer. If it doesn't work out, you can always send me back to your Uncle Grady. (Ha! Ha! Don't tell him I said that!)

You haven't seen me in a while, but I am big and fat and will be wearing a green hat and green gloves. I will have lots of hatboxes and a big blue trunk.

Thanks again for giving up your room for me!

Lots of love,
Granny Brewster

Annika Anderson stared at her mother across the breakfast table. "*Green gloves?!* I have a grandmother who wears *green gloves?*"

"Yuck!" spluttered James over his Froot Loops.

Gordon Anderson, their father, neatly sliced a banana over his cereal. "Sure! Haven't you ever heard of Granny Green-Gloves? Say, that would make a great title for a book, don't you think? *The Mystery of Granny Green-Gloves.*" Gordon was a novelist.

Annika rolled her eyes to the ceiling. "Oh, Dad!"

"For your information, Granny Green-Gloves has always believed a lady should be properly dressed," said Whitney Brewster Anderson. She was a sculptor and always used her maiden name along with her married name.

Annika, who had never seen her mother dressed up in her entire life, threw her head back and laughed uproariously. "I never heard of anyone wearing green gloves!"

A little beady-eyed skunk suddenly popped its head over the table top. "Mom, you wear green gloves," James said, offering the sniffing little creature some of his Froot Loops.

"No skunks at the table, Beeper!" reprimanded his mother. "Those are my gardening gloves you're thinking of. Granny Brewster wears *real* gloves. Soft, silky ones that go halfway up her arm. You'll see. But you must all promise *not* to laugh at her, please!"

"Yeah, Annika," said James, excusing the offensive skunk to the floor.

Annika glared at him. "What do you mean, 'Yeah, Annika'?"

"When we go to the movies, you laugh so loud, people get up and leave! It's so embarrassing!"

"I can't help it!"

"Yeah, well, maybe Granny Brewster will leave, too!"

Annika swung her legs back and forth under the table. That would be fine with her. She wasn't exactly thrilled at having this grandmother whom she'd hardly ever seen take over her room.

"How come Granny Brewster has to have my room? It's not fair," she complained.

After all, she was eleven and Thea was fifteen. For the first time in their shared lives, they each had their own room. They had moved to the Pink Farm from Seattle just so Daddy could write his detective novels in peace and Whitney Brewster Anderson could have her studio. That meant a bigger place outside the city where they could also have some land, a vegetable garden and fruit trees, some animals, and a room for each kid.

The Pink Farm was a rundown, Victorian fixer-upper fifty minutes by ferry from Seattle. It was set off the road a ways on a hill covered with Queen Anne's lace. With all the flowers and the gingerbread on the house, the setting was like something out of a storybook. But it was the color of the place that made it. The house and all the outbuildings were painted a salmon pink, the last coral hue of sunset before the sky fades to lavender. It was Whitney Brewster Anderson's favorite color.

"Perfect!" was her reaction when she first saw it.

She ran right up on the rickety porch and hugged a piece of gingerbread that had fallen from the roof.

Annika was entranced as well. "Do I get my own room?" she wanted to know.

It was the best room, too. It was the smallest of the four upstairs bedrooms, but that didn't matter to Annika. What mattered was that it had the best view. She could look out across the cow pasture and over the other wood-frame farmhouses scattered like colorful, topsy-turvy blocks around the village. Beyond the houses were the pine trees lining the shore of Puget Sound. The Sound was full of islands, like a pod of whales slumbering on the surface of the water. Annika loved to sit and watch the mist wrap mysteriously around them and the ferries weaving their way in and out the narrow passageways as confidently as ducks.

It was her own special view of the world, and she liked to write down her thoughts about it in her diary. A diary was something very private, of course, not anything she'd *ever* let anyone else know about. So she couldn't exactly make a fuss about not being able to write in it at her window.

There was, however, the subject of frogs.

"Darling, you know we've discussed all this before," Whitney was saying sympathetically. "Granny has to stay somewhere; we can't very well put her out in the barn with Prince, can we? Besides, it's only for the summer."

"She makes it sound like it's for good!"

Whitney looked to Gordon for help.

"I think Granny Brewster is feeling very lonely at the moment," he offered.

Whitney nodded guiltily. "After all, you *are* her only grandchildren and you hardly know her. Maybe she'll stay in Washington so she can be near us. But I really don't think it will work for all of us to live under the same roof indefinitely. Granny Brewster is, well, how can I say it?"

"Used to having her own way," Gordon said.

"So it's *her* idea to come here?" Annika exploded.

"Well, in a way, yes," Whitney answered evasively. "But not entirely," she added quickly.

"Then it's *her* idea to take over my room! It's not fair!" Annika yelled, pounding her fist on the table.

"Cool it, Buzz," warned her father. "How do you know? You might really like Granny Brewster."

"How do you know I might really not? After all, she wears green gloves!"

Then she remembered again the subject of frogs. Her eyes grew wider. This still had not been settled.

"And what about my frogs?"

Whitney and Gordon looked uncomfortably at each other. Annika's head turned back and forth between them as if she were watching a Ping-Pong game.

She had a thing for frogs. Her room was full of them. Fake ones, that is. Her shelves were lined with frog figurines, and all the pictures on her walls were of frogs. Her bed was covered with stuffed frogs, the biggest one being Prince Frog, as big as a beach ball with a little gold felt crown on his head.

But the best frog of all was the one Whitney had sculpted for her out of scrap metal. It was an enormous, tinny-looking thing that stood three feet high in the corner of her room. Its eyeballs and tongue, which had a fly perched precariously on the end of it, shot menacingly out of its huge head. It was enough to give any kid nightmares, but Annika loved it. She didn't know why she liked frogs. She just did.

Thea hated frogs. She liked only pretty things. Her room was painted a pale pink and decorated with a mixture of horses and theatrical posters. It was a big room on the back of the house that looked out over the woods. The view was definitely not as grand in Annika's opinion.

"You can keep your frogs in my room, Annika," James offered.

James, who was only six, had a very big heart, Annika thought.

"Thanks, Beep. But I really don't know where you'll put them all. And what about Big Frog?"

James wrinkled up his nose. "Yuck! You can keep him."

Gordon laughed. "Come now, Beeper. Don't you appreciate art when you see it?"

James sniffed. "That's not art. That's Big Frog."

It was Whitney's turn to laugh. Her family didn't quite know what to make of her talents. Something weird and wonderful could pop up anytime, anywhere. Gordon wandered into the bathroom one morning and nearly tripped over a life-size coat of armor offering him his towel. A three-foot scrap metal spider appeared in the corner of the living room one Christmas dawn. And a miniature-scale grand piano made of papier maché was being played by a suspended pair of hands as guests arrived for Annika's last birthday party.

Lately she'd started putting things on the walls that normally belonged on the floor, like kitchen chairs and other odd pieces of furniture. James especially enjoyed this newest phase and had his entire bedroom on the wall—his bed, his chair, his table, anything Whitney could tack up there. It made him feel as if he were living in space.

"Granny Brewster doesn't want to live here. She'll think we're all crazy!" Annika blurted out.

She looked at James and began to giggle. James wiggled his eyebrows. Maybe Granny Brewster wouldn't stay after all.

"Oh, no! I know exactly what you're thinking!" Whitney exclaimed, abruptly pushing back from the table. "I don't want any nonsense out of you two, do you hear me? You're to be nice and civilized to your grandmother and treat her with respect. We're going to have a quiet, enjoyable summer together. Is that clear?"

"Yes, Mom."

"Yes, Mom."

James and Annika were trying hard to straighten out their faces, but it was making them giggle all the more.

"And when she asks you something, you are to *always* answer, 'Yes, ma'am,' or you won't hear the end of it. Is *that* clear?"

"Yes, *ma'am*, Mom."

"Yes, mammy!"

"Gordon!"

Gordon leaned carefully over the table and lightly tapped his fingers. He always did that when he was about to give a lecture.

"Kids, your grandmother has been living by herself for quite some time. She's not used to a lot of noise and rambunction."

"Then how come she's coming here!" Annika exclaimed.

Gordon glanced briefly at his wife. "She's lonely. Uncle Grady has his own life. I think she really misses being around a family. So let's try and make her happy, okay?"

"Yes, Dad."

"Yes, Dad."

"Yes, Dad, WHAT?" Gordon suddenly thundered.

"Yes, Dad, ma'am!"

Their six-foot-four father was very good at turning into a horrible, child-eating monster, and he suddenly lunged at them, hunched up like a great, big woolly bear with his eyes gleaming and his tongue hungrily licking his chops.

James and Annika screamed with glee and began running around the kitchen table. Gordon chased them while making all sorts of terrible grunts and growls. Heinz, their dachshund, joined in, barking madly. Sam Ting, the Siamese cat, jumped onto one of the kitchen chairs hanging on the wall, and the little skunk dived into the broom closet.

Whitney could only lean back against the sink and

laugh. It was quite hopeless. Granny Brewster would have to take them the way they were, or not at all.

Gordon had each child squealing for mercy under his big, powerful arms. He jiggled them up and down.

"No toads in the bed?" he roared.

Annika and James were too weak with laughter to answer him. He jiggled them some more. "Can't hear you!"

"Noo!" they gasped.

"No pepper in her tea?"

"No."

"What!"

"Noo, *ma'am!*"

"Aarghh!"

"I'm going to throw up!" James cried.

"You're going to throw up?"

"Noo! I mean, yes!"

He released them gently, and they both fell back breathlessly into their chairs. They were all still laughing when the back door banged open and Thea entered— lovely, long-legged Thea, smelling of horse.

"What childish frivolity are we up to this morning?" she said, rolling her eyes in mock disgust.

Thea, whose nickname Bunny was no longer appreciated, was fifteen and beyond such goings on. She read grown-up novels and used grown-up words and had a very grown-up boyfriend who was an amateur magician with the unfortunate name of Grover Pixley. The first time Annika heard Thea mention his name in starry-eyed admiration, she laughed so hard Thea never forgave her.

"What *is* so funny?" she demanded, pouring herself a glass of milk.

"What *is* so funny?" mimicked James.

"Oh, *you* are?"

"Oh, *you* are?"

"I'm going to bop you!"

"I'm going to bop you!"

"Mother!"

"Mother!"

"Beeper, if you're through with breakfast, will you kindly take that skunk and go outside?" Whitney said firmly. "And I want that skunk to *stay* outside. No more house privileges for skunks, is that clear?"

The little bug-eyed creature peeked out of the broom closet and sniffed warily. James picked him up and hoisted him onto his shoulder.

"He can't hurt anybody."

"Your grandmother will have an absolute fit if she sees that thing in the house."

"'We need a tonic of wildness,'" quipped Gordon.

"Things are wild enough around here without skunks in the house," Whitney retorted.

"Thoreau would have loved it." Thoreau was Gordon's favorite writer. He was always quoting him.

"Yeah? Well, it's my genteel mother who's coming to stay, not Thoreau."

"Don't worry," James soothed his skunk as they went out the back door together. "I love you."

Annika wondered what she was going to do. The question of her frogs had still not been settled. Perhaps she should write another letter to Granny Brewster.

Dear Granny Brewster,

Thank you for your very nice letter. How's your packing coming along?

We are all excited you are coming. We are having very nice weather this summer so far. There are lots of nice veggetables growing in our garden like lettuce, peas, radishes, carrots, turnips (yuck!), and collyflower.

Our rabbit Lucky had five babies last week. Isn't she lucky!

Well, bye for now. See you soon!

Love,
Annika

P.S. Do you like frogs?

A week before Granny Brewster was due to arrive, Annika received a reply.

Dear Annika,

Thank you for your very sweet letter. I am all packed and looking forward to coming. This will be my first plane ride. Since I'm all packed, I don't know what I'll do for the next week and a half. Your mamma said I should get me some pills in case I get airsick, so I guess I will make a trip to the drugstore tomorrow. On Tuesday your Uncle Grady will take me to the airport and see me off. I sure hope I haven't forgotten anything!

I hope I'm not going to be any trouble to you all. Thanks again for being such a sweet girl and letting me use your room.

See you real soon!

Lots of love,
Granny Brewster

P.S. I do not like frogs really. They give me the creeps.

"Oh, well," sighed Annika, stuffing the letter back into its pink, perfumey envelope. "I'll just have to come up with another plan."

"What other plan?" James wondered.

"The Great Diabolical Granny Green-Gloves Plan."

James wrinkled his nose. "What's that?"

"I don't know. I haven't thought of it yet."

"I don't think Granny Brewster's very nice if she doesn't like frogs or skunks. Mom and Dad don't mind them too much."

"We can't let her take over, Beeper," Annika warned in a solemn voice. "I think that's what Mom's afraid of. That she's just going to move in and take over. She's already taking over my room."

"How come we've hardly ever seen Granny Brewster?"

"Well, she does live far away and doesn't like to travel. But I don't think she and Mom ever got along really well."

"Why not?"

"I don't know. Imagine having a mom who wears green gloves."

James shrugged. "Well, maybe she won't stay long."

"Yeah, maybe she won't."

Annika went to her room and, pulling out her secret diary, she began composing The Great Di—

"Thea, how do you spell *diabolical*?"

"*Diabolical?* What do you need that word for?"

"Daddy uses it a lot in his detective novels, doesn't he?"

"Are you writing *The Great Diabolical Crime Mystery of the Year*?"

"Sort of."

The Arrival

Buzzie!" Gordon hollered up the stairs. "Hurry up! We're all waiting!"

"Com-ing!"

Annika stood quietly breathing in one more time the air of her own room. In a way, it was no longer her room. Not a frog remained in sight. All the little figurines that would fit were now crammed together on one tiny shelf in Thea's room. The rest were interspersed with the dinosaurs and matchbox cars in James's room. Big Frog had descended with great ceremony to the living room where he now kept company with the spider.

But her window that opened onto her special view of the world was still there, and she gazed longingly out of it. It was a beautiful summer day, and the Sound sparkled under the sun like a bed of diamonds. Would Granny Brewster even notice?

"Buzzarooney!"

Gordon poked his head through the door and smiled sympathetically at his younger daughter. He loved both his daughters equally, but Thea had outgrown childish things. With Annika he could still be foolish and playful and not be scolded for it.

Annika looked at her father woefully. It was hard to keep tears back when he looked at her like that.

"It's a special room, isn't it?" he whispered.

She nodded and slipped into his arms. "I don't want Granny Brewster to come."

With her father, Annika could admit anything. Whitney would say she shouldn't feel like that and make her keep it all to herself. But Gordon never minded her feelings, no matter how ugly they might be.

"I know, honey," he said. "It seems very unfair, and I suppose it is. But sometimes we have to make a little extra room inside for people whether we like it or not. It's not just an outside room, it's an inside room as well. You've got your inside room all barred and bolted with a big 'No Entry' sign on the door. Let Granny Brewster come into your inside room first. Then you won't mind the outside room so much."

Annika nodded again, understanding. Her father always knew how to say things she knew to be right. That's what came of having a writer for a father. But he didn't always make sense to her or tell her what she wanted to hear.

She still felt angry and reluctant to go. But his strong, comforting arm propelled her firmly out the door and down the stairs without allowing her to look back.

As Annika climbed into the car, Whitney took one look at her and moaned. "Annika, what have you done to yourself? Can't you even *look* nice for your grandmother?"

Rule No. 1 of The Great Diabolical Granny Green-Gloves Plan: Make yourself as totally repulsive as possible.

She had put on a purple and white striped shirt over a lime green pair of shorts that had red squiggles all over them, and a pair of orange socks with her pink tennies. She leaned back with her pink rhinestone sunglasses and chomped on a piece of bubble gum.

"Annika, you look like a clown!" Thea exclaimed reprovingly.

"I think she looks great," admired James.

"How could you let her walk out of the house like that, Gordon?" Whitney scolded.

"Sorry, I thought that's what kids looked like these days."

"Yes, but she is deliberately trying to be revolting. Well, let's go. We're going to be late," Whitney huffed.

"Just calm down, Whit," Gordon said, starting up the car. "Okay, everybody ready? Let's go get Granny!"

Nobody said anything.

They stood waiting anxiously at the gate as passengers poured out of the jetway. There was no sign of a granny wearing a green hat and green gloves.

"Where is she?" demanded James, hopping from one foot to the next. Nobody else might be excited, but *he* was.

The horde of passengers began to dwindle down

to groups of twos and threes. Finally, one solitary obese woman in a blue coat came huffing and puffing up the jetway.

"Granny!" James shouted.

Before Whitney could stop him, he charged ahead, coming to an abrupt stop in the doorway. The woman glared down at him as if he were an unexpected mouse running across her path.

"Excuse me!" she exclaimed.

Gordon quickly plucked his son out of the way. "That's not her, Beep."

"I was too little the last time she came to remember," he complained.

"Did she miss her flight?" Whitney wondered out loud. She tried to grab an agent going past with a wheelchair.

"Excuse me, we're missing a granny," she said.

"I'm going to get her now," the agent said in a friendly voice.

"Oh, no, you don't understand. My mother doesn't need a wheelchair."

"Well, somebody requested one."

Whitney looked at him in amazement. "But my mother is as strong as an ox. It can't be her. Can you check and see if anyone else is on the plane? A rather big woman wearing green gloves."

"I'll check it out for you," said the agent happily.

They all watched intently as he trundled the wheelchair down the jetway. They watched even more intently as he wheeled it slowly back up. A short, stout woman in a pink coat was leaning sideways out of it. Her face was almost as pea green as her hat perched lopsided on top of a cloud of lavender hair. Her green-gloved hands were frantically clutching an enormous purple handbag, and her eyes stared bug-eyed at them from behind a thick pair of pink rhinestone glasses.

"Mother!" Whitney screeched, running down the jetway. Her horrified family followed closely behind.

"What happened to you?" Whitney demanded, leaning down to give her mother a kiss.

Granny Brewster smiled wanly up at her daughter and grabbed her hand. "Hi, darlin'. How you? Ah don't think them pills worked one bit. Ah've never been so sick in all my born days. Ah should've taken the train. Oh me!"

"Didn't you have a good flight, Mamma?" Gordon said with a chuckle, giving her a kiss.

"Y'all quit kissin' me and give me some air!"

"C'mon, kids, give Granny some room," Gordon urged.

James backed away, disappointed he hadn't been first to greet Granny. Thea kept a cool distance. But Annika didn't move, transfixed at the sight of this outlandish grandmother.

Granny Brewster smiled up at her and winked one of her giant eyeballs. "Hey there, sugah! Just look at you, wearin' all my favorite colors!"

Annika was struck speechless and remained speechless all the way out of the airport and throughout the long ride into Seattle to catch the ferry. The thought of this grandmother with a drawl as thick as pea soup coming to live in *her* room was too appalling. And even worse, James seemed to be absolutely smitten with her. This was sheer, outright betrayal. She was furious with James. He was snuggled up as close to Granny Brewster as he could get and asking her a thousand questions.

"Why do you talk funny?"

"Why is your hair purple?"

"Why do you wear green gloves?"

"Why are your eyes so big?"

"Do you know any good riddles?"

Whitney finally turned around in the front seat. "All right, Beeper, that's enough. Don't wear Granny B. out. She's had a long, hard trip."

"Beeper? You still calling him Beeper?" said Granny.

"'Cause when I was a little boy, all I could say was, 'Beep! Beep!'" explained James.

"'Beep! Beep!' I remember that! You and your daddy used to watch those Roadrunner cartoons and that's all you could say—'Beep! Beep!'"

Granny Brewster was laughing—a loud, hoarse cackle. She gave James a tight squeeze and laughed even harder. Her eyes were closed and her head thrown back, and she continued to laugh so boisterously it startled Annika.

"Good heavens, now we know where you get your laugh from," Thea whispered to Annika.

"Ha, ha!" Annika whispered back, finally thinking of something to say.

The ferry ride across the Sound was a pure delight to Granny Brewster. She seemed to have revived from her air sickness and let James drag her outside the cabin onto the deck. A stiff breeze nearly blew her hat overboard, but she caught it in time. Her lavender-tinted hair blew in soft waves against her cheeks, which were slowly regaining their more natural pink color. She gripped James's hand and patted it.

"Isn't this grand!" she exclaimed enthusiastically. "James, I think I'm going to be very happy here."

"Wait'll you see the Pink Farm, Granny Brewster. Mom's been putting chairs and things on the walls."

"She has? Well, she always was a bit peculiar, your mamma."

Annika leaned over the railing and suddenly pretended to gag.

"Dear me, are you sick, child?" asked Granny.

"Aw, she's just foolin'," said James.

"No, I'm not!" groaned Annika. "Bleahh!"

"Now why should anyone fool about being sick? It ain't funny. I should know. I felt that way all the way from Atlanta to Seattle."

"BLEAHH!"

"Mercy! Now you're making me sick!"

Granny Brewster turned and staggered back towards the cabin. Whitney and Thea hurried to assist her while Gordon and James surrounded the gagging Annika.

"Are you going to throw up?" James wanted to know, becoming somewhat more convinced.

"I-I think so," Annika said, tightly clutching the railing and squeezing her eyes shut.

Gordon rubbed her back. "You just hang on, honey, and I'll go get some towels."

As soon as he was gone, Annika peeked out of one eye. She smiled triumphantly at James.

"You *were* foolin'!" James cried.

"You be quiet about it, too, or I'll wring your neck like a turkey."

"No, you won't! I'll tell Dad if you do!"

Annika sighed. "It's a joke, okay? A secret joke on Granny."

"You made her get all sick again."

"Beeper!" Annika said, exasperated. "Whose side are you on?"

James frowned. "I like Granny Brewster. How come you don't?"

"I just don't! How'd you like it if she took over *your* room?"

"She can come sleep in my room," James said.

Annika rolled her eyes. It was hopeless. Granny Brewster had clearly won him over from the minute he set eyes on her. Well, Granny B. wasn't going to ever sink Annika with her Southern charms. Annika was going to have to wage The Great Diabolical Granny Green-Gloves Plan by herself.

It was late afternoon before they drove up the hill to the Pink Farm. The sun glowed reddishly behind it, giving it a ruby tinge. Granny Brewster clasped her hands in awe.

"Why, it's just bee-yoo-ti-ful! I had no idea, Whitney. No idea, at all."

"Wait till you see inside, Granny Brewster!" said James excitedly. "You've never seen Mom's sculptures before."

"Oh, I have, James. Believe me, I have."

Red and Toby, the two golden retrievers, bounded over to the car, determined to knock Granny Brewster flat the minute she emerged.

"Hello, hello," she said, trying to sound friendly and shoo them away at the same time.

"Red! Toby! Come here!" Thea commanded. They nosed Granny one more time and then happily bounded over to Thea. Thea ran the dog and horse show on the Pink Farm. James preferred the smaller, wilder animals like skunks and rabbits. That left Annika with Sam Ting, the Siamese cat, who could have a very nasty temper and seemed to prefer Gordon when he preferred anybody. Perhaps, Annika thought, that's why she loved her frogs so much even though they weren't real.

Whitney escorted her mother into the kitchen with the chairs on the wall. Granny Brewster looked around, somewhat dazed, and retained that expression throughout the rest of her house tour.

"Well, darlin'," she said finally, "you are one original child."

She had removed her pink coat and stood in the doorway of Annika's room wearing a purple suit with a matching purple and green scarf tied around her neck. Annika thought she looked like a giant grape.

"This is my room," Annika said quietly. "I mean, this is where you'll be staying."

Granny gave her a squeeze and stepped inside. She looked around admiringly and then went to the window and peeped out.

"My, what a lovely view! I can see the hills and the

meadows and the trees and the water—why, it's like looking out on forever!"

She turned to Annika and before Annika could blink, she squashed her in a big, tight hug. "Darlin', you don't know what this means to me. You are the sweetest girl on earth. But I can't bear the thought of you givin' all this up for me! Isn't there somewhere else—"

At that moment, she grabbed both fleshy sides of her face and let out a bloodcurdling scream. Annika felt the hair rise on the back of her neck.

"Mamma!"

"Granny Brewster!"

"What on earth?"

Granny Brewster pointed a shaking finger towards the closet. "I-in there! A-a creature! It—I—he—just looked at me!"

Gordon opened the closet and Granny screamed again.

"It's a *skunk*!"

James laughed gleefully. "Barney, what you doing in there?"

"A skunk!" Granny screamed again.

Everybody was laughing now. Except for Granny Brewster.

James picked up his pet and stroked his fur. "This is Barney, Granny. He won't hurt you."

"But it's a skunk!"

"He doesn't stink. His mother got hit by a car. Then Toby found her nest. We got the skunk people to come out and get them. They said they would de-stink one for me and I could have him for a pet. He's really friendly. Here. You wanna hold him?"

"No, no, James. I don't think so. Please. I think I've had enough excitement for one day."

"Mamma, you have a rest, and I'll send you up a cup of tea later on," Whitney soothed her, fluffing up the pillows on the bed. "Come on, everybody. Clear out. That includes the skunk."

"I don't know how he got in here, Mom. Honest!" James protested.

"Oh, I think I know!"

"I didn't put him there."

"Well, *somebody* did!"

They all turned and looked at Annika.

"What are you looking at me for?" she said, shrugging innocently.

"Because you're the only one ludicrous enough to do it," said Thea.

"Ludicrous shmudicrous!" retorted Annika.

Rule No. 2: Never admit you did anything wrong. You will then have to say you're sorry when you're really not. Never say you're sorry to Granny Green-Gloves. She will then squeeze the life out of you.

Humiliation

Annika carefully balanced the tea things on a tray and slowly climbed the stairs. It was bad enough being forced to apologize to your enemy. But to bring her tea in bed! It was the utmost humiliation.

It hadn't been easy sneaking Barney into the closet. That morning while everyone was getting ready to leave for the airport, she'd tucked the baby skunk in her blouse and made a mad dash up the stairs to her room. She'd made him a nice little bed in the closet with a cup of water and a plate of mashed-up egg in case he got hungry. Then she'd left the door ajar to give him some air. The whole time her father was telling her about her "inside" room, she'd kept worrying it might be revealed she had a skunk in that "inside" room. She thought Barney had played his part quite well.

Annika knocked on the door of her room. *Her* room and now she had to knock and ask permission to enter. Her heart began to pound. What if Granny Brewster was upset with her and told her off? She didn't know if she could take it.

"Come in," answered a tired, crackly voice.

Annika nervously brought one leg up like a stork and, balancing the tray precariously on her knee, opened the door swiftly into the room. She caught the tray with both hands just as the sugar bowl was about to slide off the edge.

"I brought you some tea, Granny Brewster," Annika mumbled.

"Oh, how nice! Do come in, sugah."

Annika surveyed her lost room. It reminded her of a fortress. Granny's huge trunk and a myriad of hatboxes were entrenched in the corner where Big Frog had been. She had peeled off her green gloves and draped them over the nightstand like a pair of long, slimy green leaves and had collapsed on the bed with one arm flung over her face.

"Oh me, if I'd a known what all I'd have to go through to get here, I don't think I would've come!"

Annika didn't say anything but looked out the window. *Her* window.

"Oh, but a cuppa tea will do me good. Thanks so much for bringin' it, sugah."

"Where do you want me to put it?" Annika asked, looking around the room for some space.

"Why, uh, move some of those hatboxes, and you can set it on the trunk."

Her whole room smelled of hatboxes, musty and fragrant at the same time. Some were square, some were round. Some had fancy braided ropes on them; others were tied with faded bits of colored string. In spite of herself, Annika was curious to see what was inside them all.

She balanced the tray on her knee again and, with her free hand, tried to remove some of the hatboxes.

"Here, you're gonna drop that thing. Give me the tray and I'll hold it," said Granny.

She was sitting up now and reaching out for the tea tray. Annika gladly gave it to her and, backing away, stumbled over a hatbox.

"Oh dear," said Granny. "I'm afraid I have too many hats. I fear they've gone out of fashion, but I've always loved hats. I've never felt dressed up without one. It's a shame, really, young ladies no longer wear hats, or gloves either, for that matter. They really make an outfit fly, if you know what I mean."

Annika wouldn't be caught dead wearing a hat and gloves. If she had to choose between wearing a hat and gloves and eating turnips, she'd eat turnips.

"Wouldn't you like to have a cuppa tea with me?" Granny Brewster asked, carefully pouring out the tea. "Oh, you didn't bring an extra cup."

"I don't really like tea," Annika said, looking at the floor. Her tongue felt paralyzed. She didn't see how she could ever say she was sorry.

"What? Don't like tea? You like iced tea now, don't you?"

"Not really."

"Well, your mamma hasn't taught you a thing, I can see!"

Granny spooned great heaping mounds of sugar into her cup and chuckled. "I like it sweet," she said as if it were meant to be a secret between them. "I'll bet you'd like it sweet. You like sweet things, don't you?"

"Yes, Granny, uh, ma'am."

"Now, lemonade. I'll bet you like lemonade." Her bug-eyes twinkled knowingly as she sipped her tea.

"Yes, ma'am, Granny," Annika replied uncomfortably. Those bug-eyes were getting on her nerves. She just wanted to get out of there.

"And fried chicken and biscuits?"

"Uh, yes—"

"Well, you just wait. I'm going to make you the best fried chicken you ever tasted. Now your mamma— she's one hopeless cook. Never could make a biscuit to save her life."

That was true. Gordon did most of the cooking. "Mom can make good pizza," Annika said, suddenly feeling the need to defend her graceless mother.

"Pizza! Oh murder, I'm afraid that kind of stuff gives me gas. I see I'm going to have to take over the cooking here. That mamma of yours! You'd never know that girl was born and raised in the South."

Suddenly a loud commotion started at the gate down below. A hoarse, somewhat incoherent voice blared up at them, "ANN'KA! ANN'KA! I GOT NEW BIKE!"

Annika jumped. "Oh no! It's Silly Millie."

"Who?"

"Silly Millie. She's this retarded girl who lives on the edge of town."

Granny Brewster set her tea cup down on the bed and heaved herself up onto her feet. Looking out the window beside Annika, she saw a large, strapping girl with long, ungainly arms hanging over the fence post. Her hair was cropped short with uneven bangs, as if she'd cut them herself. She had the body of a woman, but it was hard to tell how exactly old she was. She smiled strangely up at them.

"Dear me, hadn't you better go talk to her?" asked Granny.

The last person in the world Annika felt like talking to at the moment was Millie Brown. Somehow Millie had gotten it into her head that she and Annika were best friends. She wouldn't leave her alone. She never knocked or rang the doorbell. She yelled. And if they ignored her, she'd stay out there and keep yelling.

"ANN'KA! ANN'KA!"

Annika opened the window and leaned out. "I'M COMING!" she shouted back.

"I GOT NEW BIKE!"

"She totally gets on my nerves!" Annika exploded as she stormed out of the room. At least she'd gotten out of apologizing to Granny.

She stomped down the stairs, muttering on each step, "Why me? Why me?"

Flinging open the front door, she catapulted herself across the porch and down the steps to the gate.

"*What* is it *now*, Millie?" She never called her "Silly Millie" to her face.

Millie's happy face clouded when she saw Annika was upset with her. "I got new bike!" she exclaimed again, proudly picking it up off the ground. It wasn't new. All the paint was rusted off and the wheels were badly worn. It was much too small for her. She must have found it on a junk heap somewhere.

"Well, that's just great, Millie. Thanks for showing me. I'm afraid we're really busy right now. My granny just arrived from Tennessee, and she's really tired.

She's trying to rest. She's going to be here all summer, so *please* don't yell! Okay? It's very disturbing. Come and ring the doorbell. Can you try to remember?"

They'd asked Millie to ring the doorbell dozens of times. They even showed her how to ring the doorbell. But Millie didn't seem to remember.

"I forgot," she said gloomily.

Annika intensely disliked Millie. The girl drove her up a tree. But whereas other kids were blatantly cruel, Annika couldn't be. And for that reason, and probably that reason alone, she was stuck being Silly Millie's best friend.

"You're my *best* friend, Ann'ka, in the whole world!" Millie reminded her.

"Yes, Millie, I know. I'm afraid it's almost dinner time—"

"Tomorrow we ride bikes?" Millie asked hopefully.

"I can't, Millie. We'll probably be taking my granny around to see the sights. So don't come yelling, okay? We might not be here. And please ring the doorbell!"

Millie grasped hold of the fence post and began rocking back and forth. "Okay," she said, frowning with disappointment.

"I gotta go now, Millie. Bye." For the first time, Annika was glad she had a Granny Brewster.

"Got new bike, Ann'ka," Millie began again.

"That's great, Millie. Go home now. Good-bye."

Annika left her rocking on the fence post and hurried back to the porch. Looking up, she saw Granny Brewster peering down at her through the window.

"Why me?" she began to fume again. "This has been the worst day of my life!"

She slammed the door behind her and plunked herself down at the real piano in the living room.

"*HOME, HOME ON THE RANGE*," Annika sang out, banging away carelessly at the keys, "*WHERE THE DEER AND THE ANTELOPE PLAY!*"

Rule No. 3: Always make lots of noise. This will really get on her nerves.

Suddenly, Annika wondered if she'd made a mistake. She should have encouraged Millie to go on yelling. But no, the best way to get Millie to do something was to tell her to do the opposite.

"*WHERE NEVER IS HEARD A DISCOURAGING WORD!*"

"Annika!" Whitney stood frowning in the kitchen doorway. She had on an oversized apron and was covered with flour from head to foot. "What are you doing?"

"I'm practicing. You always say I never practice. So I'm practicing."

"I don't call that practicing. Isn't Granny resting?"

"She was until Silly Millie showed up."

"Annika, honestly, this attitude of yours has got to go! Did you apologize to your grandmother?"

Annika looked up briefly at her mother's flour-stained face and then angrily began to nibble at her cuticles. "I was about to when Millie interrupted. I had to go down and shut her up."

Whitney wiped more flour onto her nose with the back of her hand. "Look, if you're trying to be difficult, which you obviously are, you could at least expend some of your anger and go pick me some strawberries. I'm trying to make a shortcake for dessert."

"Really?" Impressed, Annika slipped obediently off the piano stool.

"And Grover's coming for dinner as well," Whitney said as if in warning.

"Grover?" Annika said loudly. "Oh, boy!"

"Annika, I don't want to hear another smart remark! Grover is a perfectly nice boy. Granny will be charmed."

"Charmed? She'll be stupefied!"

Whitney's face was beginning to go red under the flour. "Will you *please* make yourself useful and go outside and pick strawberries? I'm counting on a happy family dinner tonight, so if you can't say anything pleasant, don't bother to say anything at all!"

"Grover's not family. He's—okay, okay, I won't say a word. In fact I won't even bother to come!"

Annika stormed through the kitchen and let the back screen door slam behind her. Which was a mistake.

She took a deep breath, turned around, and slowly opened it again. Whitney was still standing there, hands on hips, glaring at her.

"Would you like to just spend the rest of the evening in bed?"

"Sorry," Annika said meekly. "I didn't mean to. It just slipped."

Whitney continued to glare, shaking her head slowly from side to side. "Try me one more time, Annika, and you *can* forget dinner."

Annika gave a little wave and closed the door with

a soft click. There was a safe side and not-so-safe side with Whitney. Slamming doors was crossing the border into dangerous territory.

She trudged into the garden where she and James had put together a scarecrow out of tin pie plates and an old pair of Gordon's brown slippers. The garden was one of Whitney's greatest delights. Annika had been given her own little plot and shared her mother's enthusiasm. But today seemed to be an exception to everything.

James was playing ball next door with the Mowatt twins. She could see their blond heads butting back and forth over the top of the fence and a soccer ball flying high in the air. James's shrieks of laughter rose with the ball and made her jealous.

James was playing a carefree game of ball, and Thea was off somewhere with Grover while she had to serve tea, put up with Silly Millie, and pick strawberries.

"What am I? Everybody's servant around here?" she muttered, plucking the ripe, red berries from their stems. "Well, they'll find out!"

The problem was being second. Thea was the oldest and a girl, and oldest girls were always the luckiest and smartest and prettiest. Unless they were the youngest, like Cinderella, and won out in the end. But being second was no good at all.

With James being the only boy, it didn't matter what number he was. He was *the* boy. There was nothing wrong with James. He didn't have to prove a thing. He could become a writer or a farmer or a dinosaur, and he would still be *the* boy.

Thea was going to be a horse trainer or an actress or marry Grover or possibly all three, but she would always be the best.

"The problem is," Annika said out loud to the scarecrow, "the problem is, I don't know what I want to be. I'm just, well, ordinary and that's why I get picked on. That's why!"

She threw the berries into her bowl in rhythm with her words. "That's why! That's why! That's why!"

Annika brought the bowl back into the kitchen where Whitney's shortcake had emerged disastrously from the oven. It had failed to rise and was as hard as a brick.

"Well," Whitney said, giving it a hard thump with her knuckles. "That's the first and last shortcake I'll ever make in this house."

"Good grief, Mom," Annika said.

Whitney's eyes lit up. "I know! I'll put ice cream and meringue on top and turn it into a Baked Alaska. Maybe that'll soften it up."

"What's a Baked Alaska?"

"You'll see!"

Grover Pixley arrived for dinner wearing shoes that shone like mirrors and a plaid bow tie. He was sixteen and had recently acquired his first car, a lemon-yellow station wagon.

"The geek's here," Annika announced.

"The what?" said Granny Brewster. She'd changed into a red and violet floral dress and ruby earrings and was sitting awkwardly in the living room next to Big Frog and the Spider like a queen in a barn.

Grover walked in, whisking a bouquet of flowers out of the air and handing them to Thea, who blushed and giggled.

"Good heavens!" exclaimed Granny. "How'd he do that?"

"Granny Brewster, this is my boyfriend, Grover Pixley," Thea said, pulling him over towards Granny.

"Hello, Grover. How nice to meet you."

"Likewise, Mrs. Brewster." Grover promptly pulled some flowers out of Granny's ear.

"What! Well, I'll be!"

Annika slunk back into the kitchen. "Grover's pulling his magic tricks on Granny," she reported to Whitney who was tossing a salad.

"Well, that should keep her out of the kitchen. I've had to run her out of here nine times."

The smell of charcoal drifted through the open windows. Gordon was busy tending the grill, and James stood adored and adoring at his side. Annika couldn't shake off her jealousy and hurriedly began setting the table.

Suddenly, "Chopsticks" resounded through the air accompanied by a chorus of giggles. Annika stuck her head around the corner, and there at the piano was Granny playing a "Chopsticks" duet with Grover!

Annika felt more than amazed; she was shocked. Grannies weren't supposed to know how to play "Chopsticks." And with Grover Pixley! It was absurd and ludicrous and ridiculous. Somehow it wasn't fair either.

At dinner Annika sat morosely picking at her grilled salmon. The Great Diabolical Granny Green-

Gloves Plan was not having the least bit of effect.
Granny Brewster was having the time of her life,
thanks largely to Grover Pixley. She laughed thunder-
ously at every one of his stupid jokes, and the stupider
they were, the harder she laughed.

But the hardest she laughed was when Whitney
pulled her Baked Alaska out of the oven. She let out a
screech and everyone went running into the kitchen.

Meringue was foaming all over the oven, spilling
over the sides of the platter and dripping into puddles
of pink gooey ice cream.

"Yuck!" said James.

Whitney began to cry while Granny laughed herself into a choking fit. The dachshund, Heinz, barking
at the excitement, began racing laps around the table.
Grover pulled a long, red hanky out of his sleeve for
Whitney to blow her nose on, and Thea and James
danced a jig together. It was up to Gordon and Annika
to mop up the mess.

"Well, how about ice cream soup for dessert?"
Gordon said, trying to cheer up his wife.

"It's not funny!" wailed Whitney.

"Mah dear, ah think . . . HA! HA! HA! . . . oh, HEE!
HEE! HEE! . . . Ah think you'd better stick to your *other*
sculpting!" gasped Granny. "Let me do the cookin'
from now on. HA! HAA!"

Grannies did not make spectacles of themselves
laughing like that, Annika told herself. It wasn't right.
She hadn't expected this sort of grandmother. What's
more, she hadn't expected . . . well, *that* wasn't true at
all!

Night
Fishing

Annika awoke to a sharp tugging on her pajama sleeve. She peered blearily through the dark into James's face hovering anxiously over her. She couldn't see him as much as she could smell his hot, sweet breath exhaling slowly into her nostrils.

"Annika?"

"What?" she whispered, jerking fully awake.

"What's that noise?"

"What noise?"

"Coming out of Granny's room."

Annika sat up to listen. All she could hear was the steady rhythm of Thea's soft breathing in the bed next to hers.

"I don't hear—"

Suddenly, there was a loud snort at the end of the hallway. It was followed by a loud rattling series of barks, whistles, and sighs so remarkable that Annika threw her legs over the side of the bed, feeling quite alarmed.

"Do you think something's wrong with Granny?" James whispered worriedly.

"I don't know."

They tiptoed down the hallway to the door where the horrible sounds were coming from.

"It's getting louder!" said James.

"Maybe we should go get Mom and Dad," Annika suggested.

"Maybe. Just in case."

They padded quickly back down the hallway to their parents' room. Quietly opening the door, they advanced stealthily towards the shadowy lumps on the bed that were Gordon and Whitney.

"Mom, Dad," they whispered urgently, standing side by side next to the bed like a pair of ghosts.

Whitney woke up with a start. "Whatisit?" she mumbled.

"It's Granny. She's making funny noises."

"Funny noises? Gordon, wake up. Granny's making funny noises."

"Hmmm?" said Gordon.

"They're *real* loud!" exclaimed James.

There was silence. Then a thundering snort resounded down the hallway.

Whitney turned over with a moan. "Oh, yeah. She snores."

"What?"

"She's all right. She's just snoring."

"Snoring!" exclaimed Annika. "I never heard anybody snore like that before!"

"Go back to bed, okay?"

"But I can't sleep!" protested James.

"Just think about something else."

"Like what?"

"I don't know, James. Count sheep."

"I don't want to count sheep."

"Then count dinosaurs. Go back to bed!"

The two of them trooped silently back down the hallway.

"I can't believe she *snores*," said James, somewhat disgusted.

Annika began to giggle. "I never heard such a racket!"

"You know what else? Her teeth come out! I saw her take them out before she went to bed."

"You're kidding!"

"Uh-uh, I'm not kidding."

"What did she do with them?"

"She had them on the nightstand, next to her glasses. I saw 'cause I went in there to say good night to her."

Annika stopped to think about this for a moment.

"Well, good night, Beeper. Hope you can sleep."

James sighed and trudged resignedly back to bed. Annika stood watching him indecisively. She had a new idea and wondered if she should tell James. He didn't seem too charmed with Granny Brewster at the moment. Maybe he'd changed his mind about her. But maybe not.

She listened to the sound of his bed squeaking on its hinges. Presently, she heard a soft, forlorn, "One . . . two . . . three . . . four . . ."

Creeping past a deeply slumbering Thea, Annika climbed out the open gabled window and up the slope of the roof. The roof was her favorite part of the house, especially at night when she wanted to look for shooting stars or listen for the faraway hoot of an owl. She sat blinking on top of the house for a moment under the clear night sky. It was studded with a myriad of stars that all seemed to be blinking back at her.

> *"Star light,*
> *Star bright,*
> *Of all the stars*
> *I see tonight,*
> *I wish I may,*
> *I wish I might*
> *Have my own room*
> *Back tonight!"*

She whispered it reverently. Wishes, like prayers, she thought, should not be said lightly. She felt very small when she sat on the roof gazing up at stars. She felt herself shrinking and shrinking until she wondered if she might disappear altogether. She wished she could disappear. It was a wish she used to make when she was James's age, convinced it could happen if she wished hard enough. She wanted to be able to disappear so she could do all sorts of fun things, like walking into strange people's houses, sliding down the polar bear slide at the zoo, and going for invisible rides on top of the porpoises that swam by in the Sound.

It never happened. In Heaven it could happen. Gordon had said he didn't see why it couldn't. By the

time she was eight, she'd had to settle for that hope.
But at least, sitting here on the rooftop, very, very still,
she could still feel as if it were happening.

She hoped she might see a shooting star because
if you wished on a shooting star, your wish was sure to
come true. She didn't think she really believed that
anymore either. But a shooting star was still a nice
thing to make a wish on.

She climbed expertly down the front side of the
roof onto the top of the porch. Granny Brewster's window
was wide open, and her snores and whistles were
blowing noisily out into the night air.

Annika peered cautiously through the window.
She could see Granny Brewster's bulky form and the
nightstand next to her, *Annika's*, bed. There was the
lamp and something boxy like a clock. Next to the
clock was what looked like a pair of glasses and a small
lump. They gleamed a bit in the shifting moonlight.

She didn't dare just crawl in and snatch them. The
floor would creak, and Granny might wake up. How to
get them? What she needed was a long pole. A long
fishing sort of pole.

Annika clambered quickly back up the roof and
down the other side into Thea's room. She tiptoed out
into the hallway and down the stairs, trying carefully
to avoid the creaks. There was a storage closet underneath
the stairs. Inside it were card tables, folding
chairs, TV trays, board games, the vacuum cleaner, a
lot of junk, and her father's fishing rods.

Annika crept inside and groped for the light bulb
string. Before she could give it a tug, she tripped
across a metal box and went crashing into a stack of

TV trays. Mortified, she clapped a hand over her mouth and froze.

It seemed the night would pass before she dared move again. She lay flat across the tables, feeling unbearably uncomfortable. Any minute now, her father would come down the stairs and flip on the light. But ages went by and he didn't come. Maybe Granny's snores had drowned out the clatter.

Finally, Annika painfully eased herself off the tables and reached for the string. The naked glare of the bulb blinded her for a few seconds. She was sure it was burning a hole through the stairs and the ceiling and shining right into her parents' bedroom.

She quickly pulled a fishing rod out of the corner without any more trouble, turned off the light, and carefully sneaked back up the stairs.

It wasn't easy sneaking around in the dark with a fishing rod. She held it straight in front of her with both hands as if it were a rifle and cautiously probed her way around the corners.

Tiptoeing past Thea, Annika guided the rod through the open window and followed after it. Without stopping to look at the stars this time, she crawled slowly up over the roof and down again to Granny's window. Granny's snores rumbled past her like waves crashing at the seashore. Annika carefully poked the fishing rod, then her head, through the window while somewhere a cricket suddenly began to chirp in unison with Granny's snores.

The rod was just long enough to reach the nightstand. Annika tried picking up the mysterious teeth with the tip of the rod, but instead, knocked them off onto the rug. She groped around with the rod for a while before finding them again. Then, scraping and nudging the teeth towards her, she finally managed to lift them up by one corner of the gums. They hung suspended briefly in the air, their pearly whites gleaming and beaming like a small sliver of the moon. Annika let out a squeak of triumph, and the teeth dropped promptly onto the floor again. Only this time they missed the rug and hit the wooden floor with a clatter.

There was dead silence. Then, "Hunhh?"

Annika didn't move. As long as she didn't move and Granny didn't have her glasses, she knew she was safe.

Nothing happened. Soon Granny began whistling like a bird. Annika breathed in relief. She quickly stretched herself across the window sill and grabbed the teeth off the floor. Stuffing her prize in her pajama pocket, she whisked the fishing rod out of the window and giggled her way back up to the top of the roof.

She wanted to laugh loud and long. Like Granny Brewster. "HA! HA! HA!" Instead, she perched herself on the peak of the house and had a good look at Granny's teeth. They were just the top teeth set into a pink plastic gum. Annika tried to imagine what it must be like to talk and chew with fake teeth in your mouth. She'd read once that George Washington wore false teeth made out of wood. She wondered if he ever got splinters and if his food tasted like tree bark.

Now that she had Granny Brewster's teeth, Annika wondered what she should do with them. She wished James was in on this with her. It would make it all the more fun, and James always had good ideas about where to hide things.

"Got it!" she exclaimed in a whisper. Trying hard not to giggle in her excitement, Annika sneaked her way back into Thea's room and down the stairs. She put the fishing rod noiselessly back into the closet and then crept into the kitchen.

Standing underneath the chair on the wall, she looked up and smiled. Perfect. With a long stretch, she reached up and deposited Granny's teeth on the edge of the seat. She couldn't wait until morning when they were all sitting around the breakfast table with Granny's teeth grinning down at them like the Cheshire cat. Annika hugged herself in congratulation. She was brilliant.

She didn't think she'd ever fall asleep and was surprised to find herself suddenly waking up to an empty room and the tempting smell of bacon. She jumped out of bed and hurried down the hallway to the bathroom. The door to *her* room was still closed. All was silent behind it.

She tried to walk casually downstairs to the kitchen, yawning extra loud so she didn't look as if she were expecting anything to happen. Gordon was all tied up in a frilly white apron that said, "Kiss the Cook," in bold, red letters on the bib. Annika kissed him. He was frying bacon while Whitney sat at the table, sipping her coffee and reading the newspaper. James, whose hair was sticking out in all directions and who looked like he'd been counting dinosaurs all night, sat slumped over the funnies.

"Oh, good morning, everybody," said Annika with another big yawn.

"Morning, sweetheart," said Whitney. "Sorry about Granny's snoring. Could you get back to sleep?"

"After a while I did." Annika stretched out her arms and glanced boldly up at the chair.

Granny's teeth were gone!

She abruptly finished her stretch and sat down. What had happened? Had they seen them and returned them to Granny already? What a disappointment to have missed it all.

"After all my hard work," she muttered under her breath.

"What's that?" asked Whitney.

"Oh nothing," Annika said. "Just muttering to myself."

"Well, please don't mutter," her mother said. "It's not a good habit."

Nobody was giving her funny looks. Not even James who had barely acknowledged her presence. Maybe they were trying to ignore the whole thing.

There was a slow thump-thump on the stairs. Annika grabbed a piece of the paper and buried her nose in it. In a moment, Granny Brewster appeared in the doorway. Annika peeked over the top of the newspaper. Granny's purple hair was frizzed all over her head, and she was wearing a bright pink housecoat and a pair of matching fuchsia slippers. She had put on her pink glasses, but something was wrong with her face. Her upper lip was missing.

"Morning, Mamma!" greeted Gordon enthusiastically.

"My teet'! I can't find 'em!" she lisped.

Annika's mouth dropped in genuine surprise along with everybody else's. What had happened to them?

"Your teeth?" said Whitney. "Where did you put them?"

"Nex' to my bed!" Granny was as bewildered as the rest of them.

"Did you look all around on the floor?" questioned Whitney.

"Evvywhere!"

The bacon and the funnies were forgotten as everybody plunged into a search for Granny's teeth. Annika quickly took the opportunity to stand on a chair and look around the wall. The teeth were definitely not there.

"What do *you* know about this?" asked a suspicious Whitney.

"I don't know anything!" declared Annika.

Then a new thought occurred to her. Sam Ting came padding softly across the floor and looked up at her cross-eyed.

"I know! Sammie took them!" Annika exclaimed.

"Sammie?" James didn't believe her.

Annika scooped the Siamese into her arms like a baby. "Okay, Sammie, tell the truth! We know you did it! You sneaked into Granny's room last night and swiped her teeth. Admit it!"

"Aah!" squeaked the cat, licking his chops.

"See! He admits it!"

"That's ridiculous," said James. "*You* did it!

Granny's door was closed. How could Sammie open it?"

"He might have gone through the window. A regular little cat burglar you are, Sammie Ting!"

"Sammie wouldn't take them. You took them," James accused. It was clear whose side he was on.

Suddenly, the doorbell rang, long and loud and clear. It didn't stop either, but continued to ring again and again and again.

"Who's that?" Annika wondered. "All right! All right! COMING!"

She and James hurried to the door and flung it open. There stood Millie Brown with her crooked grin.

"Millie!" Annika exclaimed in surprise. "You rang the doorbell!"

"Look!" Millie said, still grinning and staring at them. She opened up the dirty palm of her hand. There was Granny's pink and white upper plate covered with dirt.

"Millie, did you take Granny Brewster's teeth?" James exclaimed.

"Millie! Where? Mom! Dad! Granny Brewster!" yelled Annika.

The three of them came pounding down the stairs from Granny's room all at once. They sounded like an army of grizzly bears.

"Millie found Granny's teeth!" Annika exclaimed in disbelief.

"Where did you find them?" cried Whitney.

"I saw Heinz put them in the flowers," said Millie, suddenly aware that she had found something of importance.

"Heinz!"

They all exploded with laughter. Sam Ting must have jumped up on the chair, Annika reasoned, knocked them off, and Heinz made away with them. If Millie hadn't come along, they never would have been found.

"Well, t'ank you, Millie," said Granny Brewster, stepping forward. "I don't know how t'ey got t'ere, but t'ank doodness, you found 'em!"

"Hip, hip hooray!" cheered Whitney.

"Hip, hip hooray!" echoed Millie.

"How 'bout bweakfast, Millie?" said Granny Brewster, leading her new charge towards the kitchen.

Annika stepped outside onto the porch and watched Heinz frisk around in the flower bed. All her great plans and efforts had done was turn Silly Millie Brown into the family hero. She slumped against the railing. It wasn't fair. It wasn't fair at all.

A Discovery

"Froggie did a wooin' ride, um-hmm, um-hmm,
Froggie did a wooin' ride,
A big black pistol by his side,
Um-hmm, um-hmm.

"He rode up to Miss Mousie's door, um-hmm, um-
hmm,
He rode up to Miss Mousie's door, Knocked so loud,
He made the house roar!
Um-hmm, um-hmm.

"He took Miss Mousie on his knee, um-hmm, um-hmm,
He took Miss Mousie on his knee,
Said, 'Miss Mousie, will you marry me?'
Um-hmm, um-hmm."

Granny Brewster sat on the porch swing, swaying lightly back and forth, keeping rhythm with her song.

She was surrounded by kids. James was on her lap, a Mowatt twin sat glued on either side of her like a pair of book ends, two more were squashed on either side of them, and a whole row of upturned faces gazed up at her from the floor. Millie Brown was one of them. She was now Granny Brewster's number one fan. All the kids sang along with Granny, but Millie sang the loudest, especially on the "um-hmm's."

"Said Miss Mousie 'fore I can answer that, UM-HMM,
   UM-HMM,
Said Miss Mousie 'fore I can answer that,
I'll have to ask my Uncle Rat,
UM-HMM, UM-HMM.

"Uncle Rat gave his consent, UM-HMM, UM-HMM,
Uncle Rat gave his consent,
And they sent out the announce-ment,
UM-HMM, UM-HMM.

"Where shall the wedding be? UM-HMM, UM-HMM,
Where shall the wedding be?
Way down yonder in the hollow tree,
UM-HMM, UM-HMM."

It was driving Annika crazy. The Great Diabolical Granny Green-Gloves Plan seemed doomed. Nothing rattled Granny Brewster. Nothing. She took everything as if it were some sort of big joke. She said she didn't know when she'd enjoyed herself so much, and Whitney said why hadn't she come sooner? It seemed even Whitney was glad at long last to be reunited with her mother.

"I think I know who the prankster is!" Granny would confide loudly to James, pretending she didn't know Annika was peering into the room. Annika quickly backed out, but not before Granny had caught her with a wink from one of her giant eyeballs.

"What shall the supper be? UM-HMM, UM-HMM,
What shall the supper be?
Dogwood stew and catnip tea,
UM-HMM, UM-HMM.

"The first to come was the little white moth, UM-HMM,
   UM-HMM,
The first to come was the little white moth,
And she laid out the table cloth,
UM-HMM, UM-HMM."

Granny caught her now, peeking out the doorway. She gave her another big wink. Infuriated at being caught listening, Annika ducked inside and sped towards the back of the house. She marched outside, past the vegetable garden and down the graveled path to the salmon pink barn that was now her mother's studio.

Even though Whitney spent most of her time in her studio, she never minded her children coming there. Gordon was never to be disturbed while he was writing unless it was an emergency. But Whitney tried always to be available even if she was covered from head to foot in plaster as she was now. Somehow, she looked more dignified in plaster than she did in flour.

"Oh, hi, sweetheart," she said finally, after Annika had stood silently in the doorway for a few minutes.

Annika loved being in her mother's studio even though she didn't understand exactly what it was her mother was trying to do there. She loved the smell of paint and plaster of Paris, and the way the light pervaded the space about her as if it were an actual presence that had come into the room.

Whitney had started something new. Stacked against one wall were dozens of large sketches of what looked to Annika like flying babies. They were huge naked newborns with their eyes closed and arms outstretched like wings. They were surrounded by clouds and pairs of hands as if they were being guided through space.

On her workbench, Whitney had more sketches, plus different plaster molds of babies' heads. Annika leaned over to inspect them.

"This is weird, Mom."

"You always think I'm weird," answered Whitney.

Annika looked at her mother suspiciously. "You're not thinking about having any more babies, are you?"

Whitney gave out a short, sharp "Ha!" in response.

Annika shook her head. "That's a relief!" She held up one sketch of a baby holding out its arms towards a bird hovering over its head.

"I like this one," she said, wanting to say something complimentary.

Whitney smiled gratefully. "Do you? Yes, I kind of like that one myself."

"So what are you going to sculpt now? Babies? Mom, I don't want to hurt your feelings, but we don't have any more room on the walls."

Whitney laughed. "This is my project for the Teen Pregnancy Counseling Center. I'm trying to capture a sense of life beginning before birth, you see. A sense of movement and awareness and sensitivity. What do you think?"

"Sounds neat, Mom."

"I just hope I can get it right. I want it to be, well, you know, something really special."

Annika patted her mother on the shoulder. "It will be, Mom. Nobody can sculpt like you, that's for sure."

Whitney looked seriously at her daughter. "What about you? You don't look like you're enjoying life much."

Annika shrugged. "I'm not."

"Oh, Annika," sighed Whitney, frowning. "What am I going to do with you? Where are all the others?"

"Granny's singing songs to the whole neighborhood again."

"So why are you being an old stick in the mud?"

"I'm not some little kid anymore!" Annika fumed. "I don't sit around singing baby songs." She began imitating Granny.

"Froggie did a wooin' ride, um-hmm . . . "

To her dismay, Whitney laughed and sang on after she stopped.

"Froggie did a wooin' ride,
A big black pistol by his side,
Um-hmm, um-hmm!

"Oh, those aren't baby songs. They are the songs of my youth. I never get tired of hearing them."

"I thought you hated being from the South."

"I did once."

"But not now?"

"No. I wouldn't go back. I like where we are. But I don't have bones to pick anymore. I've made my peace."

"How? What bones?"

Whitney sighed again and picked up one of her baby molds. "Oh, you know. I grew up when there were bones to pick about everything, especially in the South. I resented it being so backward, so racist. I thought my mother was a hopeless relic of the past. I wanted to become her total opposite, and I have. But now all that doesn't seem to matter too much anymore. The funny part is, my children are all just like her. You especially."

Annika opened her mouth in horror. "I am not!"

"I'm sorry. I shouldn't have said that. But I'm afraid it's true. And you're doing everything in your power to keep from loving her. Like I did."

"Well, I don't love her! I can't stand her! She's driving me nuts!" Annika exclaimed, trembling. "I don't seem to belong here anymore, I can tell!"

"Oh, Annikins," protested Whitney. "I was only trying to let you know I understand, somehow. But don't you think Granny's really quite a lot of fun? Don't you think you'd enjoy her if you really tried? I don't think you've tried."

"She doesn't like me anyways," said Annika defiantly.

"Of course she likes you! She wouldn't have come if she didn't like you."

"Well, she likes James better. She even makes a bigger fuss over Silly Millie than me."

Whitney shook her head. "That's not at all fair, Annika. And I don't like hearing you call Millie Brown, 'Silly Millie.' Please don't let me hear it again. Is that understood?"

"Yes, ma'am."

"Come give me a hug."

Annika gave her mother a perfunctory hug and left the studio feeling grumpier than ever. The sky was overcast, and a thin veil of mist enveloped the trees around the farm. There wasn't much of a view today. Altogether, it was a very gray and melancholy day. She didn't usually think of it that way; she preferred "cozy and mysterious." You could do something with words like that. But today was just plain "gray and melancholy." There was no hope for it being otherwise.

Annika stopped to inspect her vegetables. The rabbits had gotten into them again. There were munch marks on the lettuce and radish tops. Her tin plate scarecrow had stood dull and useless while the little pests helped themselves.

Annika sighed in frustration. What to do? From the front porch, she could hear a second round going of "Froggie."

"Next to come was a big black snake, UM-HMM,
    UM-HMM!
Next to come was a big black snake,
And he ate up the wedding cake!
UM-HMM! UM-HMM!

"Froggie come a swimmin' 'cross the lake, UM-HMM,
    UM-HMM,
Froggie come a swimmin' 'cross the lake,
And he got eat up by that same black snake,
UM-HMM! UM-HMM!"

Annika couldn't sympathize with any song in which gallant little frogs got eaten up on their wedding day. But it gave her an idea. She mounted her bicycle and rode into the village.

She was having to be sneaky now whenever she went out on her bike. The minute she hit the road, Millie seemed to appear instantly behind her on her "new" bike.

"Ann'ka! Wait! Wait for me!" Millie would holler. And along she'd come, wobbling and weaving with her face set in a concentrated grimace of determination.

There was no shaking her off either. Annika would ride as fast as she could, only to be followed by a shrill wail, "Ann'ka! Wait for me!" Exasperated, she would slow down and urge her on.

Annika congratulated herself this time on having avoided Millie altogether. Millie was so busy singing her lungs out, she didn't even notice her best friend sailing down the driveway past her. But no sooner had Annika reached the gate on her return than Millie pedaled frantically up on her bike. She quickly took in that Annika had a package and had been *somewhere*, and her bottom lip began to quiver in disappointment.

"Let's ride bikes, Ann'ka," she said hopefully.

Annika shook her head. "Sorry, Millie, I've just come back."

"Why?" asked Millie.

"I had to go to town. You don't always have to come with me, Millie. You're not a good enough rider."

"Am too!"

Annika wondered what on earth had ever possessed Millie's parents to let her ride a bicycle. It was dangerous for someone like her, wasn't it? Maybe they didn't care. Annika didn't really know them. Nobody did. They were elderly and simple-minded themselves.

"Millie, I think you better go home now," Annika said firmly.

Millie looked away and began to cry.

"Now, don't cry, Millie!" Annika said impatiently. "I'm not going to ride bikes with you today. I don't have to ride with you every day, okay?"

Large, blobby tears were rolling down Millie's ugly, contorted face, and her nose began to run as well. Annika clutched her dime store bag. Then she suddenly thrust it at Millie.

"Here, you want to see what I went to get? Open it."

Millie gulped and sniffed and took the bag. Hoping to find candy, she eagerly opened it.

"Licorice?" she said at first. She started to put her hand in, then violently jerked it back. Her face blanched in horror, and she quickly shoved the bag back at Annika.

"And it will eat you up just like Froggie if you don't go home right away!" Annika said crossly.

Millie turned her bike quickly around, and sobbing loudly, lurched unevenly down the road.

Annika watched her go. She felt horrible. It was wrong to be mean to someone like Millie. She knew that.

She slowly wheeled her bicycle through the gate and saw Granny Brewster all dressed up, standing on the porch steps with her fists on her hips.

"What's wrong with Millie?" she asked.

"Nothing. She's just being a baby because I won't ride bikes with her. I'm too tired now."

"Well, I hope you talked sweet to her. I don't think she's looked after right."

"Where are you going, Granny?" Annika asked, trying to hide her guilt by changing the subject.

"Your mamma's taking me to get my hair done. It's a mess."

"Well, see you later then."

Annika steered her bicycle around to the back and then deposited her purchase in the vegetable garden. "That'll take care of you varmints," she said, shaking a finger at whichever of them might be listening.

She sauntered slowly back into the house and up the stairs. She felt horrible and guilty, and suddenly curious. Granny was out of the house for a while. It was a perfect time to do some investigating. She opened the door to her old room and tiptoed in.

Rule No. 4: Never feel guilty. It will make you miserable.

Annika surveyed the hatboxes stacked inside the closet.

Rule No. 5: As a last resort, hold Granny Green-Gloves' hats for a ransom of six hundred bucks.

Annika began opening the hatboxes one by one. She expected to laugh at their silliness, but instead she was startled. They were the most beautiful hats she'd ever seen. There were broad-brimmed straw hats with ribbons and flowers, hats covered with silky little veils, velvety, mushroomy hats studded with jewels, feathered hats, sequined hats—hats a queen would wear.

Annika felt bedazzled by them all. One by one, she started trying them on. She lifted up a satiny red hat with a single white silk rose nestled on its brim and angled it carefully on top of her head. It was the most beautiful hat of all.

Admiring herself in the mirror, she thought herself anything but ordinary. Her eyes sparkled, her skin took on a glow, and her pale, wishy-washy sort of hair curved artfully under her chin.

"It's like magic," she murmured softly. "I must be gorgeous."

"What are you doing?" James the policeman stood frowning in the doorway.

"Oh, Beeper, aren't they elegant?" she whispered.

"Those are Granny Brewster's hats. You better not touch them."

"You won't tell, Beep, will you? I just want to try them on, and then I'll put them right back. She'll never know."

"You might get them dirty."

"Oh, you're such a fuddy-duddy, James Anderson. You're no fun anymore. Ever since Granny Brewster came, you've been a—a hopeless relic of the past."

James wrinkled his nose. "A what?"

"A dinosaur, James. A raggedy-toothed old dinosaur."

"If they find out you've been playing with Granny's hats, you're gonna get it!"

"Oh, shut up, James! Why don't you think Granny wears any of these hats?"

"You're not supposed to say, 'shut up.' It's not nice."

"But, James," Annika sighed, feeling the day's gray and melancholy frustration coming back to her, "aren't they beautiful? And she never wears them."

"You'll get in trouble," James warned again, walking away.

Annika carefully folded the yellowed crinkly tissue back over each hat. They must be worth a million. But she'd forgotten about holding them for ransom. In fact, she'd forgotten what a gray and melancholy day it was and that she'd purposefully been mean to Millie. She'd forgotten what she'd put in the vegetable garden. In fact, she'd forgotten all about The Great Diabolical Granny Green-Gloves Plan. For the first time in her life, she'd discovered what it was like to feel beautiful.

A
New Plan

Granny Brewster found the snake in the vegetable garden. She went out to pick some lettuce for a salad and came back screaming.

"Whitney! Gordon! There's a—a snake in the garden! A big—black—snake! Where's a hoe?"

James was all eyes and ears. "A *snake*, Granny B.?! We've never had a snake before!"

"It might be poisonous, so don't go pickin' it up, James."

"Maybe it's the same black snake that ate up Froggie, Granny B.," James said excitedly as he bolted down the back steps.

Gordon went after the hoe, and Whitney armed herself with a broom. As she passed Annika, she noticed a slightly suppressed smirk on her daughter's face. She abruptly set down her broom.

"I suppose you're behind this," she said with a gasp. "Honestly, Annika Anderson, a snake?"

Annika shrugged innocently and rushed outside, followed immediately by her mother. Gordon was carefully tiptoeing with his upraised hoe through the vegetable patch. James and Granny were close on his heels. Granny was gesturing frantically while her new cone-shaped hairdo pointed up and down like a torpedo searching out its target. The sight of them all made Annika suddenly bend over double with laughter.

"It's fake!" she hooted. "Boy, did I ever fool you! HA-HA-HA!"

They all turned around, startled. No one laughed, or even smiled. They turned back around and crouched to have a better look. Gordon gave it a poke with the hoe and then picked it up by the tail. A long, rubbery black snake dangled harmlessly from his fingers.

"Why, you little bamboozling boogie, it is a fake snake!" he said, looking up with a mean grin on his face.

"Oh, murder!" exclaimed Granny, a bit sheepishly. "It sure looks real!"

"Oh, Annika, you and your jokes," said James, greatly disappointed it wasn't a real snake.

"'Oh, Annika,' is right," said Whitney, not at all pleased with her daughter's behavior.

"'Bout gave me the fright of mah life," Granny said, breathing heavily. "Shew! I think ah better sit down."

Granny's eyes suddenly rolled back in her head, and she sat down right on top of the lettuce leaves.

"Mamma!" Whitney cried, hurrying to grab her. "Are you all right? Gordon, she's fainted!"

Gordon grabbed her as well, while James hopped excitedly from foot to foot. "Is Granny all right? Is Granny all right?" he kept saying like a stuck record.

Annika felt stricken. "I didn't mean to scare Granny. I didn't mean to scare anybody except the rabbits. Honest!"

Granny's eyes were half-closed, and she kept nodding her head and mumbling. Annika was sure she'd killed her.

"Mom, is she gonna be all right? Please, I didn't mean it."

"Come on, Mamma," Whitney urged, struggling to heave her hefty mother to her feet. "We've got to get her inside, Gordon."

"I know, but I'm afraid I'm not going to be able to carry her."

"She's not going to die, is she?" Annika blurted, her panic level swiftly rising. Who ever heard of a kid killing her own grandmother?

"Let's just get her in the house," Whitney commanded.

All together, they tried to form a human lever to wedge Granny out of the lettuce leaves. They strained and struggled, but each time Granny seemed ready to get up, she toppled back again.

"This isn't going to work," Gordon said finally.

"Well, we can't leave her here!" Whitney expostulated.

"Is Granny going to die in the lettuce patch?" James began to sob hysterically.

"Oooh, ooh, I'm all right, y'all, I'm all right," Granny mumbled breathlessly. Her eyes were squeezed shut, and she had a funny smile on her face as if she wanted to laugh, but couldn't.

"Here, let's try the wheelbarrow," Gordon suggested.

"Wheelbarrow!" Whitney was indignant. "You can't put my mother in a dirty old wheelbarrow!"

Gordon hurried over to the garden shed where a grass-encrusted wheelbarrow was propped up against one side. He wheeled it over and promptly began trying to hoist Granny into it.

"What's wrong with a wheelbarrow? I don't know how else to get her out of here, Whit. Heave, ho!"

With one great push, they managed to land Granny in the wheelbarrow. She gripped the sides and gave out a chuckle.

"Oh, murder! I'm sorry, y'all. Mah knees are just turned to water. Ah'm afraid there's one thing you should all know. Ah *hate* snakes!"

"I'm sorry, Granny. I didn't mean to scare you. Please forgive me," Annika pleaded. "And please don't say, 'oh, murder!'"

Granny's eyes popped open. "Good heavens, child, don't carry on so. I'm fine! No snake is gonna be the end of me if I can help it!"

"Hang on, Mamma!" Gordon picked up the handles of the wheelbarrow and, with Granny holding rigidly to the sides and the rest of them holding onto Granny, he trundled her out of the garden and up the graveled path to the house.

At this moment, Thea and Grover drove up in the

lemon yellow station wagon. They both leaned out the windows with their mouths hanging open.

"Why's Granny in the wheelbarrow?" Thea demanded.

"She fainted!" James explained eagerly. "Annika put a fake snake in the vegetable garden and Granny found it!"

The wheelbarrow ride somewhat revived Granny. "Whee!" she laughed. "I haven't ridden in a wheelbarrow in over twenty years!"

"What? You used to ride them often?" Gordon asked.

"Oh, hush. It was a Sunday school picnic. Granddaddy and I entered one of those wheelbarrow races, and we won, too!"

"Let's give Granny B. a ride all around the farm!" James suggested enthusiastically.

"Oh, no!" said Whitney as they helped Granny up the steps. "Granny B. is going inside and have herself a peaceful dinner. And I don't want any more practical jokes scaring the life out of her, is that clear?" She looked directly at Annika.

"I was only trying to scare the rabbits!" Annika defended herself. "They've been eating the lettuce again."

"Rabbits or no rabbits, I don't want any more practical jokes."

"It wasn't a practical joke!" Annika exclaimed.

"I don't care. Enough is enough!"

Annika felt miserable the rest of the evening. What had turned out to be the best and totally unplanned Granny Green-Gloves plan wasn't giving her the least bit of satisfaction. To make matters worse, Granny was being especially sweet to her and enticed her into a rousing game of Parcheesi. Granny beat everybody at Parcheesi. She was an expert at board games and greatly relished her victories.

This made Annika all the more miserable. *She* always used to win at Parcheesi. And *she* didn't slap the table and go "HA-HA!" every time she knocked somebody home. Well, maybe not quite as loudly as Granny did. *She* certainly didn't gloat over being the champion, unbeatable until Granny Brewster showed up.

Afterwards, Thea and Grover drifted out onto the porch, and James snuggled up in Granny's lap with a giant-sized version of *Grimm's Fairy Tales*. Gordon and Whitney decided to take the dogs for a moonlit walk. The clouds had unraveled across the sky like cotton, revealing the moon's existence.

"Want to come, Buzz?" Gordon asked.

Annika shook her head. She knew they'd rather be alone. "No, thanks. I'm tired."

"Rapunzel! Rapunzel! Let down your hair!" Granny croaked like a witch, making James laugh.

Annika watched the two of them wistfully for a moment. She suddenly wished she were James's size and could cuddle up like that. Granny looked up at her, then quickly back at the book.

"Annika! Annika! Let down your hair!" she said in a deep, heavy voice.

"What!" exclaimed James. "It doesn't say that!"

"Oh, yes. Rapunzel's real name was Annika. But only the prince knew it, you see."

"No, it's not. You're making it up, Granny B."

Granny looked up at Annika again, only to see her flee up the stairs.

"Well, now, there is a little princess named Annika who's got herself quite stuck up in a terrible old tower," Annika heard Granny say. "How do you think we can get her down from there?"

Annika didn't know. She crawled through Thea's bedroom window and over the roof to the other side. A thin layer of mist had covered up the half-moon like gauze. The half-sphere of light looked lonely, incomplete without its other half, as if it too were tucked behind the window of a tall, impenetrable tower.

Down below, Annika could hear Grover murmuring something poetical to Thea—something about the moon as well.

"I love you, Thea," she then heard Grover say in a manly voice.

"I love you, too, Grover," Thea gushed shyly.

"Oh, brother!" Annika announced herself loudly.

There was a stillness, then a giggle, then two heads appeared from underneath the porch.

"Annika!" Thea gasped. "What are you doing up there?"

"I spy a little spy," scolded Grover playfully.

"Enjoying the moon, same as you." Annika sighed with exaggeration.

"Annika, you're being a brat, you know that?" said an exasperated Thea. "You've become absolutely impossible. Now go back inside."

"But I like it up here. Boy, nobody seems to want me around anymore."

"Well, I should go anyways, my fair goddess," spoke up Grover. "You need your beauty sleep."

What a goon! How could Thea stand him, much less *love* him?

"Ah, 'parting is such sweet sorrow'!" Annika moaned theatrically.

"Yes, indeed it is!" Grover answered back with a short wave.

Thea followed him to his car, kissed him good night, and watched him slowly drive down the road. Without looking up at Annika, she sauntered dreamily back into the house.

Annika felt all her loneliness and gloom come over her again. The night was quiet except for the rushing of the wind in the tops of the pine trees. What should she do? Clearly, she must do something. She didn't belong here anymore. Everybody fit in, except her. Even Granny Brewster with her Southern drawl and purple hairdos seemed to have found her place at the Pink Farm. But Annika? She just seemed to be in everybody's way.

"It's 'Oh, Annika!' this and 'Oh, Annika!' that," she sighed unhappily. "I think they're all tired of me."

Suddenly, under the silver gauze of the moon, an owl with outspread wings lifted up from the top of the tallest pine tree. It flew in an arc over the silhouetted rooftops of the village, then flapped languidly off towards the woods in back of the farm.

Annika watched it keenly. "It must be a sign," she mused out loud. "I should follow it." Deep into the heart of the woods where nobody could find her—a secret hiding place—with a view, of course.

She could have her frogs again, too. She would become a frog scientist. She would make all kinds of important discoveries. Maybe she'd even be famous someday! Like that guy who lived in the woods—what was his name?

The revelation of it all was so exciting, Annika could hardly contain her sudden rapture.

Annika Josephine Anderson, world-renowned frog scientist, spent several years living and studying in the woods near her Washington home. Because of her faithful work, frogs today are appreciated and admired the world over.

Ecstatic, Annika clambered back over the roof and through Thea's window. Even Thea's hard look as she entered could do little to topple her excitement.

"Really, Annika, you are incorrigible," Thea said, propped retiringly against the pillows on her bed. "Can't you behave decently for once?"

"Oh, sniff! sniff! 'I love you, Grover, dah-ling!'" Annika teased.

Thea threw a pillow at her. Annika threw one back with all her might. It burst open in a cloud of feathers all over Thea.

"Annika!" she exclaimed, spitting feathers out of her mouth.

Annika laughed, and so did Thea.

"Thea's the Snow Queen! And Grover's the Snow King!"

"What's that supposed to mean?" Thea said, coughing out more feathers.

"You're *not* going to marry him, are you?" Annika asked.

"Who knows?" answered Thea with a shrug. "I hope someday."

"Oh, gag! Not *him*, Thea!"

Thea was busy sweeping feathers out of her bed. "Look, it's none of your business!" she retorted. "Get over here and help me clean up my bed."

"Well, I intend to have *swarms* of boyfriends, not just one," Annika informed her grandly, blowing a handful of feathers into her face.

"Well, I'll take Grover, thank you. He's good and sweet and kind like Daddy."

"*I'm* going to be famous. That's why I'll have so many boyfriends."

"Oh, really?"

"I'm going to become a great scientist and write lots of books like that guy who lived in the woods. You know, Daddy's favorite writer he's always quoting from."

"Thoreau?"

"Yes, him."

Annika bit her tongue. She'd expose her whole secret plan if she wasn't careful.

She was too excited to sleep. She remembered seeing something in her father's study. It was something Thoreau wrote about living in the woods. What was it?

Once the house was quiet, except for Granny's snoring, Annika sneaked quickly downstairs with her diary and pencil. Her father's study off the kitchen was always a mystifying place. It smelled of leather and books.

Annika turned on the green-shaded desk lamp

and let her eyes roam over the dozens of quotations framed and pasted on the wall above it. Many of them were by "the guy who lived in the woods." Finally, she found the one she wanted.

> "I went to the woods because I wished to live deliberately, to front only the essential facts of life, and see if I could not learn what it had to teach, and not, when I came to die, discover that I had not lived.
>
> *Walden*, Henry David Thoreau"

Annika read it again and then copied the quote into her diary with a feeling of awe and anticipation. She wasn't really sure what it was supposed to mean, but she had a feeling it was something great.

"'I went to the woods because I wished to live,'" she whispered solemnly to herself. Well, she certainly couldn't live here anymore.

"I'm going to live," she wrote in her diary. She stopped to chew on her pencil eraser for a minute. Then, "It'll be the best thing I ever did."

Into
the Woods

"What's that?" Annika said with disgust.

James and the Mowatt towheads, Andrew and Austin, were busily stirring a large washtub full of mud, twigs, and leaves.

James looked up at her reproachfully. "It's dogwood stew, that's what!"

"Dogwood stew?" Annika laughed loudly. "Whatever put that—oh, I get it! That silly song about froggie and mousie."

"It's not a silly song!"

"What *is* dogwood stew, anyways?"

James gave the mud a slow, thick stir. "It's what frogs eat, Granny said. So we're makin' some to catch frogs with. Only we don't have any dogwood. But Granny B. said applewood was just as good."

Annika stiffened. "You can't catch frogs with that muck." After all, *she* was the future world-famous frog scientist.

"I think it needs more bugs," said Andrew thoughtfully.

Austin quickly produced a jar of dead flies. "Here, I caught some more flies."

"Oh, great!" said James. "Dump 'em in."

Austin shook them out over the tub with a firm slap on the bottom of the jar. "There they go!" he exclaimed as they peppered the stew.

"Oh, gross!" Annika stalked away.

"Where are you going?" James called after her as she climbed the fence into the pasture.

"None of your beeswax!" Annika answered back importantly.

She was quite sure they wouldn't watch her. They were already bending their blond heads back together over their dogwood stew, earnestly discussing what to toss in next.

"Dogwood stew!" she muttered to herself as she sidestepped the cow pies. "I suppose they'll be making catnip tea next."

Granny Brewster had certainly done a thorough job of brainwashing every kid in the neighborhood. Except her, of course, Annika Josephine Anderson, world-famous frog scientist. She didn't have time for such nonsense. She had far better things to do with her life than being stuck in the middle of everything and belonging nowhere. Today was the day she was going to begin to *live*.

It wasn't a very different sort of day to begin with than the previous day or the day before that. They had had nothing but drizzle and more drizzle for the past three days. Annika had postponed her search for a place to live in the woods, hoping for a nicer day, until she realized she could come to the end of her life waiting and yet not have lived.

The drizzle had at least toned down to a very moist feeling in the air. The pasture grass was a vivid green, and the cattle stood chewing it thoughtfully and somberly, their damp, red hides and muddy hoofs making them look a bit bedraggled. It was actually a very good day for frog observing.

Annika watched her step carefully, not just because of the cow pies, but in case a frog should happen to hop her way. It was part of her new plan: Annika Anderson's Great Scientific Frog Discovery Plan.

Rule No. 1: Always be observant.

She was feeling very observant today. She had a small notebook and pencil tucked inside her jacket pocket, and, pulling them out, she began to take notes every few steps.

"Good frog-hunting conditions today. Cloudy, wet sky. Wet grass. Wet cows. Wet, drippy trees. Wet mud. Frogs like it wet."

"No frog sitings yet."

"Still no frogs."

"Frogs are good at hiding, I bet."

Annika climbed over the fence at the back end of the pasture and slipped nonchalantly into the woods. She was sure no one saw her, but just in case anyone did, she wanted it to appear as if she were doing something very normal, and not going off to live in the woods.

But who cared anyways? No one would even miss her. They wouldn't notice she'd been gone, most likely, until she was world famous and they realized it was her, Annika Anderson from the Pink Farm. Then they would all feel so miserable for not even missing her that they would all plead and beg for her to come back. Why, she could even have her very own room back!

Annika became so preoccupied with her visions of fame and fortune that she didn't pay attention to where she was going. There was a sudden drop-off onto the road that ran through this particular part of the woods. It wasn't steep, only muddy and slick. Annika wandered dreamlike through a silvery grouping of giant alders when suddenly the ground disappeared from underneath her. She went zinging straight down into a gloppy puddle of thick mud.

"Ohhh!" she wailed. "Ohhh!" She was covered with mud. It had even splashed up into her hair.

"My notebook!" she wailed even louder. "My brand new notebook!" It had flown out of her pocket and landed squarely in the mud in front of her. She picked it up gingerly and tried to wipe it off in the grass. But the grass was wet and only smeared it.

"Oh, what a catastrophe!" she moaned.

There was nothing else she could do except go home and change her clothes. And buy another notebook. Maybe living in the woods wasn't all it was cracked up to be.

"Well, I won't give up!" she said out loud as she tried to stand up. "I guess becoming a frog scientist will not be so easy."

There was a sudden crack behind her, as if a tree branch had fallen. Or as if somebody had stepped on

one. Annika turned around. The trees were silent once
again.

Annika sighed, re-pocketed her notebook, and
tried to climb back up the embankment. She had
wrenched her foot in the fall, which was making it difficult. She sat back down and tried to rub it.

As she sat there rubbing, she heard horses clop-
ping down the road. In a few minutes, Thea and Grover
appeared, sitting royally astride their horses and
laughing. They weren't laughing at Annika. They
didn't see her until they were right next to her. Annika
wished desperately she could fall into a hole somewhere. But as there wasn't any hole or any other place
to hide, she tried to assume as dignified an air as was
possible while sitting in mud.

"Annika Anderson!" shrieked Thea, suddenly
realizing it was her sister she was staring at. "What
happened to you?"

"I was out walking, and I just happened to fall
down in the mud, can't you see?" Annika replied as
calmly as she could without looking at either of them.

Thea and Grover both dismounted and came over
to inspect her. "Are you hurt?" Thea asked anxiously.

"No-o-o, I'm quite fine," Annika said proudly.

"Here, we'll help you up," Grover said, offering
his hand.

The last person in the world Annika wanted to be
rescued by was Grover Pixley. "I don't need help," she
answered quickly. "I am quite fine. I've just been resting here a bit."

"If you're fine, then why are you rubbing your

foot?" asked Thea. "Come on, we'll give you a ride home."

"I don't need a ride home," Annika insisted. "Please don't let me spoil your ride. Besides, I'm quite enjoying myself here, you know. I can hear the birds singing and look up at the trees—"

"Oh, baloney!" cried Thea. "You've obviously hurt your foot, you're covered with mud, and here you sit saying you're enjoying yourself! Let us help you, for pete's sake."

Thea and Grover both grabbed an arm, and Annika reluctantly let them pull her to her feet. After all, she couldn't very well sit in the mud all day rubbing her foot. It couldn't be very useful to a frog scientist, except it gave her some idea what it was like to be a frog. Of course! In school last year, they'd seen a film about a lady who studied gorillas in Africa by acting like one.

Annika was so excited by this new revelation that she hardly noticed it was Grover's horse she was being hoisted onto. Her humiliation had its redeeming value after all.

She was met back at the Pink Farm with all kinds of fuss and bother. Whitney immediately plunked her into a hot bath which seemed to do wonders for her foot. It wasn't swollen, and, no, she didn't want to go see a doctor, thank you. She could walk on it fine now. Whitney thought it should be taped anyways, and James and his friends admired her bandaged foot with much envy. Granny Brewster declared a good, hot, Southern fried chicken dinner was what she needed to build up her strength.

Maybe she'd been wrong about leaving home. But to give up her life's calling after only one try? No, she would never let anyone call her a quitter. If there was anyone to call her that.

"Ribbet!" she croaked in James's ear just as he was biting into his drumstick.

"Ow!" he said with a jump.

"Ribbet!"

He couldn't keep from giggling. "What are you doing?"

"Ribbet!"

"Did you hurt your brain as well as your foot?" James asked, poking Annika with his drumstick.

"I think she must have," said Thea, helping herself to more mashed potatoes. "She's turning into a frog."

"Ribbet!"

"Well, now, I thought there was a sweet little girl sitting there a minute ago," said Granny Brewster, helping herself to the mashed potatoes as well.

"She wants a kiss," said Gordon. "Grover, give her a kiss and she'll turn back into a little girl."

"Don't you *dare* try and kiss me!" Annika warned, jumping up from the table.

"See, I told you!" said Gordon, laughing heartily.

"Did you thank Granny for her great dinner?" Whitney whispered in Annika's ear later on as they were clearing the table. "I think she'd appreciate it if you gave her a big hug."

"Granny B., that was a wonderful dinner," Annika said, giving her a wide berth. She wasn't about to get hugged. "Thanks for cooking it."

Granny put down her scouring pad and wiped her hands on her apron. She had tears in her eyes. "Well, anything for mah sugah girl."

It was too late to escape. She wrapped her fat arms around Annika and gave her a squeeze, squashing Annika's face into her huge bosom. It wasn't exactly comfortable getting your face mashed into a giant-sized bosom. If her bosom ever got that big, Annika thought she would die of embarrassment. It was a tremendous relief when Granny finally let go of her.

James seemed to thrive on such hugs. He was constantly throwing himself into Granny's ample arms and loving the life out of her. This continued to irritate Annika until she realized what bothered her was that James had simply exchanged his affection for her to Granny Brewster. Not only had her room been taken away from her, but James as well.

Annika's heroic homecoming was short-lived. The next day she was just plain, ordinary Annika Anderson again. Gordon had his new novel to write, and Whitney was filling her pink studio with flying babies. Thea remained absorbed in Grover and Prince the horse. And James and his buddies quickly went back to inventing dogwood stew.

"It's time to carry on," Annika determined. "The summer will be half over and I won't have discovered a thing."

She went back to the woods, this time carefully wrapping her new notebook in a plastic bag. Again she went in the direction of the great owl with her heart and mind full of dreams and observations. But this time, she kept an eye open to where she was going.

How did you follow the flight of an owl? Annika wasn't really sure. And where did an owl build its nest in the woods?

"Way down yonder in the hollow tree," she suddenly found herself singing. The song lodged itself in her mind and wouldn't go out of her head. She began singing it further without meaning to. It somehow had a grip on her.

"This is going to drive me crazy!" she said out loud. "I'll have to sing something else."

Annika could never remember all the words to songs. She preferred making up her own, instead. She started singing to the tune of "Turkey in the Straw":

> "Oh, I'm a little froggie
> And a froggie is me,
> And off we go,
> We froggies we,
> And if we come back,
> Well, I don't care,
> Cause my mousie
> Got eaten by a bear.
>
> "Oh, froggie and me
> Froggie and me
> Ya-dum-dum-dum
> Dum-dum-dum-dum,
> Oh, that funny froggie and me."

She thought it was pretty good and laughed out loud to the tops of the trees. The fragrant firs and graceful alders surrounding her were quiet in response. Only the wind occasionally touching their branches made them sigh or nod. She listened to the sound of her own footsteps crunching on the pine needles, and then she noticed something odd. There was a faint echo to them somewhere in the background. When she stopped, they stopped.

Annika turned around. She could see no one, hear no one. It must be her imagination. She didn't think anything more of it for the rest of her walk. But the more she explored, the more she had a funny feeling someone was following her.

Princess Josephine

Annika found the hollow tree quite by accident. She had ridden her bike along the shore road at the bottom of the village hill when a flock of crows shot out of the road-side firs as if from a cannon. Their flapping wings and magpie squawking made such a racket Annika wondered what had frightened them.

She steered her bike off the road into the pine trees and found a little path that went down to the water. Funny, she'd never noticed a path before. And she was sure she'd been in and through these trees a dozen times. Intrigued, Annika pushed her bike along the path.

She could see nothing that would startle a crow. The multiple tiers of fir branches concealed only the sky, and their fallen needles covered only the rich, dark ground. She breathed in the fresh, pungent scent of pine and sea and eagerly pushed her way down to the water's edge.

The waves of the Sound lapped gently over a few abandoned fish. Someone must have caught them from the weathered log lying next to them and then just left them. Or maybe the sea had deposited them itself.

Annika propped her bike against the log and sat down. There was no beach, only a thin strip of mud that curved around the trees. But from where she sat, she had a good view of the Sound and its islands. Suddenly, Annika realized she'd found her place.

"This whole wood will be mine. The log will be the front porch, and this is the passageway to all my secret rooms. But one room will have to be the most secret of all."

She spent the rest of the afternoon exploring further along the shoreline and in and out of the trees. She wandered finally into a small circular clearing nearly covered from view by what looked like low-hanging fir branches. Then she realized a tree had fallen over. It had snapped in two, making a kind of curtain out of its dying branches and leaving a hollowed-out stump.

"A hollow tree!" Annika exclaimed with excitement. She wondered if the owl lived here.

"I'll bet he does live here," she thought aloud. "It's beautiful and mysterious and why wouldn't he? Even if he doesn't, I can pretend he does. I'll call it The Owl's Nest."

Annika looked around for a sign of the owl, but it didn't look like anything lived here. Except the trees.

"Oh, well," she declared, looking up, "henceforward, this place shall be known as 'The Owl's Nest of the Whispering Trees,' the place where Annika Josephine Anderson made her greatest discoveries, and when she came to the end of her life, she realized she had not lived in vain!"

A sharp crack of leaves and pine needles jerked Annika out of her reverie. She twirled quickly around and peered through the branches. Was somebody spying on her? She never saw anyone when she looked. No footprints, no telltale signs. Except the crows. Something or *someone* had startled them.

She shook off the feeling. She wasn't afraid. It was a friendly village, and there were houses all around the woods. Still if she were going to accomplish anything and not be bothered by spies (if, in fact, there were any spies), then she needed to be much more secretive.

She looked up. Straight up. Why couldn't she build a house *in* the trees, the same as an owl? The fallen pine made a perfect ramp up to the bottom branches of another fir tree. Its low, flat-spreading branches would be perfect for a lookout.

Annika climbed up the dead tree and then, grabbing hold of the live tree next to it, swung herself up into the crook of a fir branch. "Wow!" she breathed, taking in the view. She quickly wrote in her notebook, "Today I have found the PERFECT place to begin my great discoveries about frogs."

Suddenly, Annika realized something else. Most frogs did not live in trees. They lived in ponds. How was she going to discover anything about frogs up here in a tree?

The Great Scientific Frog Discovery Plan Rule No. 2: Find out where frogs live.

Rule No. 3: Stick to your plan.

She was not sticking to her plan very well. But it was certainly much nicer sitting up in the branches of a fir tree looking out over the Sound than it would be mucking around in a smelly old pond. Annika sighed dreamily. It was just as good as having her own room back again. She could start looking for frogs tomorrow.

Annika returned to The Owl's Nest the next day and every day after that. Her frogs would have to wait until she'd finished building her house. Even if she lived in a tree, she could always go and investigate ponds later on. And there were such things as *tree* frogs, after all. Maybe she should zone in on them.

Annika sneaked something new out to The Owl's Nest of the Whispering Trees every day. She picked out short scraps of lumber from behind the shed, hammer and nails, a small oval rug, her frog collection, and a tin of cheese and crackers. She hammered the boards together and made a little platform for herself in the tree. The rug softened up the wood, and the cheese and crackers gave her something to nibble on. The frogs gave her company.

It had all been very thrilling and amazingly easy. However, now that she'd finished her house, something was missing. She wrote it down in her diary.

Rule No. 4: A scientist should be daring and bold and never have any fears about anything!

What had she done that was daring and bold? Anybody could build a house in a tree. What she needed was *inspiration*. That was what her dad said he had all those quotes up on the wall for and what

Whitney loved about the color salmon pink. It *inspired* her, like the colors of the sunset rewarding you for a day's work done.

Annika tried to think of what it was that inspired her. Frogs? Sunsets? Music? No, it had to be something *very* special.

She thought and thought until, suddenly, she knew. It would be very daring and bold of her to obtain it. It would be downright diabolical. That would make it all the more worthwhile.

She waited for Whitney to take Granny out for her next hair appointment. James was busy playing outside. Thea was off on her horse. Gordon was locked up in his study, and Silly Millie had miraculously stayed clear of her ever since she'd been scared off by the fake snake. Annika felt as if she had the world to herself.

She sneaked softly into Granny's room and opened the closet door. Above her, on the shelf, were neatly stacked rows of Granny's hatboxes. One by one, Annika lifted them down. She opened them all up until she found the one she was looking for. The wide-brimmed red satin with the single white silk rose.

"She'll never miss it," Annika said, placing it majestically on her head as if it were a crown. "Your Royal Highness, Princess Annika. That doesn't sound right. Your Royal Highness, Princess Josephine. Yeah!"

She quickly packed the hat back into its box and then rearranged the others back on the shelf. With the box ribbon over her arm, Princess Josephine descended the stairs, holding her other arm out to all her imaginary royal subjects and blowing them kisses. She swept and bowed her way serenely through the invisible crowds lining the hallway and spilling over into the kitchen. Then, with one last genteel wave, she stepped carefully out the back door and, seeing no one, made a mad dash for her bicycle.

Annika sat in her lookout, wearing the red satin hat on her head and nibbling cheese and crackers. She felt every bit the princess of the forest. She forgot to look for tree frogs or any other kind of frogs. She was too busy having imaginary conversations with her royal stuffed frogs. But she filled her diary daily with all the inspiring things she saw or felt about the world, and it all seemed to her the grandest thing she had ever done.

She imagined and wrote stories about the people who rode by on the ferries and fishing boats every day. One day, a different sort of ferry with a different sort of passenger floated past her. It was a logjam occupied by a circus of barking sea lions. Some lazily basked; others played tag in and out of the water, while others just sat there and barked and wagged their flippers. Annika laughed and barked back at them.

There were gray and melancholy days as usual, but more often the midsummer skies were a continuously changing shade of blue. Pale white-blue, a greeny eggshell blue, and the brightest, freshest, boldest shade of blue there could ever be.

The colors of the water changed, too—richer shades of blue, green, and gray reflecting the colors of the sky and always as if someone had freshly painted them. Life for Princess Josephine was peaceful and tranquil again.

Until one day the hat disappeared.

Annika felt cold fingers of horror grasp at her throat and stomach. She always carefully put the hat back in its box and wrapped it in the rug to keep the box dry. Then she hid it in the hollow tree stump along with the cracker tin and piled leaves over it so it looked perfectly like a tree stump, hiding nothing. But now it was gone!

The cracker tin had been emptied and cast aside in the woods. Annika scoured every inch of the clearing for the hatbox and hat, but there wasn't a trace of it.

She slumped miserably in a heap onto the ground. Who would have taken it? Who had seen her? She had been spied upon!

"It just goes to show you," Annika said aloud, not at all sure what she meant.

Now, what would she do? She couldn't call the police. She had taken Granny's best hat without asking, and now someone else had taken it. Even if Granny never missed it, it was still her hat.

But what felt worse was that someone had also taken away her inspiration. No one should ever be allowed to steal somebody else's inspiration. *When you have lost your own room and your inspiration, it just goes to show you,* Annika thought, *how bad things can be sometimes.*

She sighed and sighed again. There was nothing else she could do but go home. It was not a pleasant prospect.

That evening she sat like a stone at the dinner table.

"What's wrong with you?" James asked. "You're all grumpy again."

"I am not!"

"You sure *sound* grumpy!"

"So what's wrong with being grumpy once in a while? Everybody gets grumpy. I'll bet even the President gets grumpy!"

"Are you feeling all right, Annikins?" Whitney asked sympathetically.

"She looks a bit feverish," declared Granny. "Maybe some hot lemonade—"

"*Hot lemonade!*" Annika exclaimed. "Oh, gag!"

"It's what my mother always gave me when I felt sick," Granny continued.

"I don't feel sick!"

"Just grumpy," said James.

Annika looked at him sorely. Once she could have told James anything with perfect confidence. But she wasn't so sure she could now. She badly needed to confide in somebody, and James was always good at finding things. She needed his help.

Annika stayed grumpy the rest of the evening, for which she finally got sent to bed early. This was fine with her. It gave her time to crawl out on the roof and try and think of what to do.

"Dear God," she sighed, looking up into the murky night sky. It wasn't any use wishing on stars. This time she needed to pray.

"I hope You're listening 'cause I'm afraid I'm in *real* trouble now. I took Granny's best hat without asking, which was bad of me, and now it's been stolen by someone else, unless a wild animal found it and ate it. But I don't think any wild animals live around here anymore that would eat a hat. So please, *please* help me find it, and I'll promise to put it right back, cross my heart and hope to die, amen!"

Annika felt a little better. But she thought her prayer lacked something.

"And, dear God, *please* may I not come to the end of my life and discover I have not lived."

That sounded a lot more inspiring, Annika thought with satisfaction. Shivering, she suddenly decided to crawl back inside and tell James.

She tiptoed into his room and climbed the rope ladder up to his bed. His arms were flung back above his head and his mouth was wide open. He looked so funny she hated to wake him up.

"James!" she whispered, giving him a nudge.

"Hmm?" he said with a smile.

"James! Wake up, Dopey. I have to tell you something important."

He opened his eyes and grimaced. "What is it?"

"You have to promise me you won't breathe a word to Granny or Mom or Dad."

"I won't," he said, propping himself up on his elbows. "What is it?"

"I've lost Granny's big red hat, and you have to help me find it."

"*You* lost Granny's hat!" he said loudly.

"*Sshhh!* It could be anywhere. We have to try and find it."

"But how'd you lose it?"

"I can't tell you. But maybe whoever took it is playing a joke and left it somewhere. In the woods or a barn or a field. I need you to help me look, okay? And if you find it, I'll give you a reward."

"What?"

"Ice cream."

"Chocolate?"

"Any kind you want."

"Okay. Ice cream and—"

"What else?"

James always had his own price. "Root beer."

"Okay. Root beer."

"And—"

"And what else?"

"An elephant ride."

"An *elephant* ride!"

"I never rode one before."

"Well, I can't promise you that, James!"

"And some Fig Newtons for Barney," he added.

Annika nodded. "Fig Newtons for Barney. I hope I can remember all this."

The next day James enlisted the help of the Mowatt twins, and with visions of ice cream and root beer followed by elephant rides, they took to the woods beyond the Pink Farm.

Annika eagerly rode her bicycle back to The Owl's Nest. Maybe whoever took Granny's hat had brought it back.

She peered hopefully into the hollow tree stump. No hat had been returned. Disappointed, she made another search through the woods. She was about to give up when she heard a loud snap.

A Tragedy

Annika screamed. A wild, hideous face bore down on her own. She was so frightened by it, it took her a few seconds to recognize whose it was.

"Millie Brown!" she gasped. "You could have killed me!"

Millie Brown sat up, her lower lip protruding in a thick pout. Pine needles were sticking out of her hair and clothes, making her look like a giant porcupine. Annika stared up at the tree from which Millie had suddenly dropped.

"What were you doing up in that tree, Millie Brown?" Annika demanded. She slowly stood up and brushed herself off.

Millie moaned and rubbed the pine needles out of her hair.

"*You've* been spying on me!" Annika accused angrily. "You've been following me all around, and now you've eaten my cheese and crackers and taken Granny's hat! I know you have, so don't deny it!"

Millie's lip extended even further. "I didn't do it!"

Annika stared at her. "Yes, you did!"

"I didn't!"

"You did!"

"I didn't!"

Exasperated, Annika pulled at the sides of her hair. "You are such a liar, Silly Millie!" she exploded. "You are a snoop and a thief and a liar! What have you done with Granny Brewster's hat? It doesn't belong to you, and we are all going to be in big trouble if you don't give it back!"

Millie burst into tears. Great blobs of tears gushed in force from her eyes like a river. Then she threw her head back and bawled like a little kid.

"I didn't do it!" she wailed. "I didn't do it!"

It was horrible to hear someone cry like that.

"Oh, Millie, stop it! Stop, please," Annika begged.

Millie shook her big head. "I didn't do it! I didn't do it!"

"Okay, okay, Millie, calm down," Annika ordered, deciding to try a new tactic. "Okay, you didn't do it. Maybe you can help me find it then. If you find it, I'll . . . I'll buy you some ice cream. How's that?"

Millie began rubbing her eyes, taking in large gulps of air and hiccoughing, like a motor sputtering and winding itself down. Annika looked at her hopefully.

Then Millie reared back her head and scowled fiercely. It was an expression Annika had never seen before.

"No!" she said defiantly.

"No?"

"You called me 'Silly Millie.' You're not my friend anymore!"

With that, Millie awkwardly stood up and stomped off through the trees. Bits of pine needles still clung to her back and the seat of her pants.

Annika watched her go, feeling a mixture of shock and anger. It was the first time Millie had ever stood up to her or anybody.

"Hey, Millie, wait a minute. I didn't mean it. Honest."

Annika started after her, not any less convinced Millie had the hat, but keenly aware she had snapped some invisible boundary line. It made her suddenly afraid.

"Millie, wait!" She began running, but so did Millie. She had hidden her bike near the road under some leaves in a ditch. Snatching it up with a peculiar strength, Millie swung her leg over the seat and pedaled furiously down the hill.

"Millie!" Annika yelled. "You're going too fast."

Scared, she ran back for her own bike and raced down the hill faster than she had ever gone herself.

Millie was careening wildly all over the road. She was clearly out of control, but she kept going faster.

"Millie, slow down!" Annika shouted after her. But she might as well have been yelling at a bullet.

There was an intersection at the bottom of the hill. Annika suddenly saw a car approaching the stop sign. It made a momentary stop, then pulled ahead. Annika gave one last scream.

When the driver saw Millie, it was too late. She slammed into the side of the car and went flying over the hood.

Engulfed in horror, Annika skidded within inches of Millie's crumpled bicycle. She flung down her own bike and tore around the front of the car. Millie lay sprawled unconscious in the ditch with one leg twisted underneath her.

"Millie! Millie!"

The driver and his companion, both elderly, were shaking violently. "I didn't see her! I really didn't see her!" the man said, his voice breaking. "She just came out of nowhere."

"I'll go get help," Annika assured them, her own body shaking more than she could control.

People were already running from yards and houses, and Annika screamed at them. "Help! Please call for help! A girl's been hit!"

One woman nodded at her and quickly ducked back inside her house. Annika hurried back to Millie. She was lying so horribly still.

By the time the police and ambulance arrived, a small crowd had gathered around the accident. James and the twins had also heard the commotion, and when they discovered it was Millie Brown who had been hurt, they raced home to tell their parents.

"Is she okay?" Annika asked tearfully as the paramedics lifted Millie's limp body onto a stretcher.

"She's still alive," one of the medics assured her kindly. "We'll do our best."

"Her name's Millie Brown," Annika told them. "She's retarded."

The Anderson station wagon pulled up just as the ambulance began to pull away. The police were asking Annika and the driver all sorts of questions. The minute Gordon leaped out of the car, Annika flew terrified into her father's arms.

"Oh, Daddy! Millie Brown got hit by a car, and it's all my fault!" she sobbed.

"Annika!" cried Whitney, racing around the front of the car. "Are you hurt, darling?"

"No, but Millie—oh, I just want to die."

"Now, hang on! Hang on, honey. What's the story?" Gordon said in a strong, soothing voice.

"The girl came out of nowhere," the elderly driver repeated for the hundredth time. He was worried his license might be taken away. "I've had a perfect driving record for sixty years. Nothing like this has ever happened to me before!"

"I was mean to her," Annika continued to sob. "She was spying on me, and I got mad at her. She took off on her bicycle, but she was going too fast. I tried to stop her, b-but I c-couldn't!"

"Calm down, sweetheart. It's going to be okay," said Gordon. He looked at the policeman. "Is the girl hurt badly?"

"She was knocked unconscious. Your daughter said she's retarded, but doesn't know her age or her parents. Can you give us any idea who to contact?"

"Her parents are elderly," Whitney said, looking involuntarily at the distraught driver and his wife.

"Where are they?" Granny Brewster suddenly demanded from the back seat of the car where she was forcibly detaining James and the Mowatt twins.

"I'm afraid we really don't know anything about her parents," Gordon explained.

"Well, it's high time then, I'd say!" Granny exclaimed. "Y'all quit goin' on about whose fault it is and go find her parents, for heaven's sake!"

Suddenly, Granny Brewster was in charge. She ordered her family back into the station wagon, and with a hastily arranged police escort, they all took off down the road.

Millie's house was hidden from sight at the end of a long, rarely traveled dirt road. Nobody ever went near the place, but everybody knew where it was by the strange, rusted iron bedstead that stood at the entrance to the road. It was a common prank at Halloween to paint it neon orange or putrid yellow. If anyone dared. Old Man Brown supposedly prowled around the place with a shotgun.

The little boys in the station wagon stared wide-eyed with a mixture of fright and curiosity as they bounced past the iron bedstead. Flakes of garish orange paint from a previous Halloween were peeling off of it. They had now passed the point of no return, and even a police escort was no security against what monsters were supposed to inhabit the Brown place.

The house was in a state of near collapse. It was stripped bare of any paint, and holes in the windows were covered up by yellowed sheets of old newspapers. The porch had almost entirely caved in under the weight of broken-down furniture and discarded appliances. Garbage was everywhere, piled up to the windows and obscured only by the height of the weeds that surrounded the entire house.

Granny emerged out of the car, her face one bright red blister of rage.

"Look at this! Will you look at this? I knew that girl wasn't bein' looked after right. We should've come over here a lot sooner."

Everyone else looked around in shock. The policeman approached them, scratching the back of his head.

"I've seen some dumps in my day, but this one takes the cake."

Granny marched through the weeds up to the porch when a low, beastly growl suddenly issued out of the splintered floorboards. A large, wolfish-looking dog with a face like a gargoyle followed the sound, struggling out of its black hole just in time to prevent Granny from going any further.

"Oh, good heavens!" She stared at it, placing her hands indignantly on her hips. "What a *horrible* dog!"

Annika looked around in disgust and fear while holding tightly to Gordon's hand. James was clinging to Gordon's other hand, while each of the Mowatt twins had grabbed hold of one of Whitney's arms. Somehow human contact kept the nightmare of Millie Brown's home from coming too close.

So this was where Silly Millie lived. In a garbage dump. Annika suddenly saw a shred of newspaper peel away from the window and two sharp eyes peer through the glass. She shuddered. Whatever existed beyond that front door was hard to imagine.

There was the sound of keys jangling, bolts being unbolted, and locks being unlocked. Minutes seemed to pass before the door barely opened and a shriveled-up stick of a woman with mousey gray hair poked her head through the crack. She took in the crowd of people with the policeman standing in her front yard, and her eyes grew dark with fear.

"What is it?" she croaked in a hoarse voice that seemed unused to speaking. The dog growled once more, but she ignored it.

"Are you Mrs. Brown?" Granny Brewster asked politely.

"Yes," the woman snapped. "What's happened?"

"Your daughter Millie's been in an accident on her bicycle."

"Millie?" Mrs. Brown opened the door wider. "She ain't got a bicycle. What are you talking about?"

"She's been ridin' around on one for weeks," Granny said indignantly. "Didn't you know? She's just been hit by a car and taken to the hospital. If you like, the policeman's here to escort you over there. He also needs some information from you about Millie."

Mrs. Brown's face shriveled even further. "Oh, no!"

There was a slight shuffling behind her, and a man, unkempt and unshaven, suddenly appeared waving a double-barreled shotgun.

"What's goin' on here? Git off my property!" he bellowed.

The policeman quickly stepped forward, his hand on his gun.

"Oh, put that away, you old fool!" Mrs. Brown ordered. "Millie's been hurt. She's in the hospital."

"I'll kill 'em! I'll kill 'em!" Mr. Brown threatened.

"Shut up, Ben! Just shut up and go lie down."

"Do you have transportation, Mrs. Brown?" the policeman asked, keeping a wary eye on Ben.

"Yes, there's a truck out back."

"If you and your husband would like to follow me, I'll see you get to the hospital all right."

"I'll kill 'em! I'll kill 'em!" Mr. Brown shouted over his wife's shoulder.

"No, you won't neither!" scolded his wife. "Don't mind him, Officer. He's touched in the head. He ain't never hurt nobody."

Nobody. Except Millie.

Annika stared down at her hands. They'd all hurt Millie.

A Question

Annika had been sitting on the porch roof for quite some time. The sympathetic *who-who* of a lonely owl echoed across the meadow, but she wasn't really listening. She wished she could pray or even make a wish. But the few stars she could see looked cold to her in their distance tonight. All she could do was sit there and shiver.

A shadow appeared at the window above her. She didn't notice it until she let out a sigh and the shadow gasped.

"Who's out there?" came a harsh whisper from Granny.

Annika's heart jumped. "It's just me, Granny B. Annika," she answered in a forlorn voice.

"What on earth are you doin' on the roof?"

Annika hugged her knees more tightly and shrugged. "I like it on the roof."

There was a pause. Then Granny said sharply, "Aren't you cold out there?"

"Nooo," Annika said, trying to keep the shivers out of her voice.

"Mind if I come join you?"

"What?"

"Mind if I come join you?"

"But, Granny B.—"

"I know. You think I'm too big and fat and old to sit on a roof. Well, I'm not in my grave yet."

She stuck one round leg out of the window, then the other. Annika quickly reached up to help her. "But, Granny B., what if you fall off?"

"Hush! I'll do no such thing." She stepped gingerly onto the porch roof and then eased herself slowly down next to Annika.

"Whew! It's cold out here. I suppose you get a good view of the stars though."

"Sometimes, when it's clear."

"What you thinkin' about?"

Annika stared at this grandmother of hers sitting on the roof next to her. "Oh, nothing much."

"You just like sittin' out here all by your lonesome?"

"Why not?"

"I think that's what's troublin' me, darlin'. You're too much by your lonesome. You need to talk about what's troublin' you. If you don't, you'll grow up to be one unhappy girl. Your mamma was like that."

Annika looked again in disbelief at the cone-shaped silhouette sitting beside her. "What do you mean?" she asked, her curiosity aroused. Whitney never talked much about her youth to her children.

"She always kept everything inside of her tight as a drum. I could never get a word out of her. Maybe I tried too hard, or maybe I tried the wrong way. But one day she just exploded, said, 'Mamma, I'm leavin',' and packed off to New York. Just like that. We didn't hear from her for quite some time. She was 'findin' herself.' I thought she'd lost herself. But that was the thing your mamma's generation had to do. Find themselves. It doesn't seem to me like they found much. Winifred had a bad time of it, I think, until she found your daddy instead. He helped her pull out of herself."

"Winifred?"

"Didn't you know your mamma's real name is Winifred?" Granny sounded surprised.

"No!"

"Well, don't go tellin' her I told you. She was named for my mamma, but it never suited her. She always hated it. She changed it to Whitney the minute she left for New York. It was like she wanted to erase everything including her name. But there's a part of her that's still Winifred and always will be."

Annika felt shocked. "Winifred! My mother's real name is Winifred?!"

"Well, it's not as bad as that. She's still your mamma, whatever her name is. Perhaps I shouldn't have told you. But it does tell you something about your mamma. And me. I think she's finally beginning to come to terms with who she is. It's why I've stayed away so long. To give her space. But it seems to me we ought to need each other a bit more. It's not good bein' alone all the time. I found that out when your grand-daddy died."

Annika fidgeted with the hem in her pajamas. A lump like pie dough was rising up in the back of her throat. It was true. It wasn't so good always being alone. Sometimes it was good. But not when you had bad feelings boiling around inside of you. Being alone just made it worse.

"Do you think Millie is going to be all right?" she asked, her voice catching.

"I think so," Granny said with a positive note to her voice. "The doctor says she had a concussion and a broken leg. People recover from those things, and Millie's a big, healthy girl. It'll take time. But you need to quit feelin' sorry about what happened and concentrate on what you can do for Millie when she gets better."

"But—but she's hurt her head." This had been worrying Annika most of all. "Do—do you think she'll be even *more* retarded?"

"I think Millie has a lot more goin' for her than people realize. When you see where she's come from, it's a wonder she's not worse!"

"I was so mean to her, Granny B. I never meant to be. I just was."

"Well, I suppose I'm the one who upset the apple cart to begin with. You've been angry at me for pushin' you out of your room, and it's set you on edge ever since."

Another wave of guilt and remorse washed over Annika. She buried her face in her hands. "Oh, Granny,

I've been so wicked. I'm the wickedest, meanest girl there ever was. I don't think I can ever be forgiven."

"Sure you can," Granny retorted. "I was a lot wickeder than you and I was forgiven."

"How were you wickeder?"

"I set the school on fire once," Granny said matter-of-factly.

Suddenly, Annika laughed. "On purpose?"

"No, not on purpose. I wasn't that wicked. I snitched some firecrackers from my brothers and just thought I'd have me some fun while the teacher was out of the room. Well, I lit one and it caught the curtains on fire. Just like that, the whole room was full of smoke and all the kids were screaming. Fortunately, we all got out and no one was hurt. But a lot of damage was done, and we had to finish out the school term crammed in with the sixth graders.

"I was considered a very wicked child after that, and no one would play with me or invite me to any parties. I was quite devastated as I wasn't used to having to play by myself, and I just loved goin' to parties. I finally gave my own party, but only one little boy showed up, and his mother made him. That was your granddaddy."

Granny suddenly grew quiet. "Well, I haven't remembered about that part in a long time. But I had a Sunday school teacher, Miss Gracie Stone, who said she was still my friend and so was Jesus. I figured if someone as good as Miss Gracie still wanted to be my friend, then maybe Jesus did, too. And I reckon He was."

Annika stared up into the night sky. She was shiv-

ering uncontrollably now. She wanted to go inside to
her warm bed and go to sleep. But then morning
would come, and perhaps she'd find everyone was
blaming her for Millie's accident after all. No one
would want to be her friend anymore.

She looked up at Granny. Granny Brewster, her
mortal enemy, wasn't blaming her for anything. Back
up in the night sky, the stars were beginning to twinkle a bit. *I wish I may, I wish I might* . . .

"Aren't you freezin'?" Granny wondered.

"Ye-e-es." Annika moved crablike across the slate
and tucked herself gratefully under Granny's outstretched arm.

"Look at the stars," Granny said, as if reading her
thoughts. "It's a lovely view."

"Yes, it is," Annika admitted, suddenly bursting
into tears. "Oh, Granny B., I'm sorry. You don't know
how mean I've been to you."

Granny chuckled and hugged her close. "Believe
me, darlin', I know. I'm not as dumb as I look."

"Granny, I didn't want to come to the end of my
life and find out I hadn't lived!" Annika blurted.

"What?"

"You know how Daddy loves to quote Thoreau?
That guy who lived in the woods and became famous?
Well, that's why I was in the woods and why Millie
came spying on me and why—"

Somehow, she couldn't quite confess yet about
the missing hat. Maybe there was still hope of finding
it.

Granny chuckled some more. "Goodness, child,
you don't have to go runnin' off to the woods and live

like a hermit. Sounds like your mamma runnin' off to New York. 'I've gotta live my *own* life!' Seems to me there's plenty of livin' goin' on right here. Isn't that why y'all came out here? Not that that makes it any easier. Sometimes it's just plain work."

Annika felt strangely comforted. Somehow it seemed the most natural thing in the world to be sitting and talking on the roof with Granny Brewster. She laid her head sleepily against her grandmother's ample bosom. Granny began to rock and hum until the deep-throated humming turned into words.

> *"Why should I feel discouraged? Why should the shadows come?*
> *Why should my heart be lonely? And long for heaven and home?*
> *When Jesus is my portion, My constant friend is He,*
> *For His eye is on the sparrow, And I know He watches me,*
> *His eye is on the sparrow, And I know He watches me.*
>
> *"Blessed assurance, Jesus is mine,*
> *Oh, what a foretaste of glory divine,*
> *Heir of salvation, Purchase of God,*
> *Born of the Spirit, Washed in His blood.*
>
> *"This is my sto-ry, This is my song,*
> *Praising my Savior all the day long,*
> *This is my sto-ry, This is my song,*
> *Praising my Savior, All the day long."*

"That's what your mamma's tried to run away

from. Don't you go runnin', y'hear?" Granny murmured softly in her ear.

"I won't, Granny," Annika promised.

"It won't do you no good, no how. Once He's got you in His grip, He don't let go. Like that owl out there. I know."

"Has He got me in His grip, Granny B.?"

"Well, only you can answer that. Has He?"

The air was still, as if waiting. Annika looked up at the stars and the night shadows that covered them. She thought of the pine trees, the owl in flight, and the words of the old hymns that came from places and times she'd never known. And she wondered.

An
Answer

Millie turned her face away and refused to look at Annika. Her leg was encased in an enormous cast and was suspended in the air by all sorts of wires and pulleys. She looked like something out of a cartoon.

"Millie, I wish you'd talk to me," Annika pleaded. "I wish you'd forgive me so we can be friends again."

Millie's thick lip continued to point up to the ceiling as if it too was in traction.

Annika sighed helplessly. "I guess you hate me."

She walked out the door to where her family sat waiting. Millie turned her head and watched her go.

"It didn't work," Annika announced gloomily.

"Won't she talk to you at all?" asked Whitney.

Annika shrugged and drooped her shoulders. "Nope."

Granny gave her a tight squeeze. "Well, don't give up, darlin'. Keep tryin' and she'll come 'round eventually."

"I don't think so. She looks pretty miserable."

"I think *you* look pretty miserable," said Granny. "That's not gonna help any. You gotta be real sweet and cheerful and make her forget how miserable she is. She'll just feel more miserable if you are, too."

"That's right, honey," agreed Gordon. "Why don't we all go back in and give her a big cheerful good-bye."

"I know," said James with sudden inspiration. "Let's sing her the 'froggie' song. She really liked that song."

"Good idea, Beep," said Gordon. "Let's all sing the 'froggie' song."

"I don't know the 'froggie' song," protested Thea.

Gordon gave her a playful shove through the door. "Well, you're about to learn it, Bunno."

"Millie, we're all going to give you a big *cheerful* good-bye and sing you the 'froggie' song," James informed her with the biggest, most cheerful grin he could muster.

"Froggie did a-wooin' ride, um-hmm," they all began, sounding flat.

"Y'all can sing better than that!" Granny reprimanded. "Line up and stand straight. That goes for you too, Millie. Ha-ha! Just kiddin'."

They tried it again, but it took a couple of verses before they got going, each verse rising further on the cheerful scale. Millie just glared at them.

"Come on, Millie!" James broke in halfway. "UM-HMM! UM-HMM! Don't you remember it anymore?"

The two other patients who shared the room clapped and urged her to join in as well. Millie stared up at the ceiling and ignored them.

"Piece of corn bread on the shelf, Um-hmm, um-hmm,
Piece of corn bread on the shelf,
If you want anymore,
You gotta help yourself,
UM-HMM! UM-HMM!"

They all smiled their most cheerful smiles and waved good-bye. But Millie remained as stuck as her thick lower lip.

"Well, you can't say we didn't try," Annika said as they left the hospital.

"The problem with Millie is her spirit's been broken as well," said Granny. "The child needs encouragement. If she doesn't get it, she'll probably think she'll never walk again, much less ever ride another bicycle."

"She really loved that bike of hers," said Thea thoughtfully. "It's like falling off a horse. Remember the first time I fell off Prince and broke my arm, Daddy? I never wanted to ride again, but you made me. You said I'd be skittish for life otherwise, and the only cure was getting right back on where I left off, so to speak."

"Of course," Whitney chimed in. "The only way that girl will ever really recover is by riding a bicycle again."

"But she hasn't got one anymore," said ever-practical James.

"Mrs. Brown didn't even know she had a bicycle," pondered Whitney. "I wonder where she found it."

"They've got so much junk, maybe it was just lying around somewhere," James suggested.

Annika remained silent. It was all up to her to restore Millie's spirit. She was the one who'd broken it. Millie had always tried to copy everything she did. She was responsible for the way Millie was now.

"We'll have to make a plan," she said, more to herself than the others. And because she happened to be good at that sort of thing, she set to work thinking up one.

The Great Millie Brown Bicycle Plan
Rule No. 1: Get a bike.
Rule No. 2: Give Millie the new bike.
Rule No. 3: Get Millie to ride it.

It was a very simple plan, as far as Annika's plans usually went. But to get a bike cost money. And to get Millie to ride it wasn't going to be very simple at all.

It was James who came up with the money idea. He and the Mowatt twins came bursting into the kitchen shortly after breakfast one morning. Barney was hanging onto James's shoulder for dear life.

"We—caught—a—frog!" James exclaimed breathlessly. "It worked!"

"What worked?" asked Whitney.

"The dogwood stew!" James's face beamed with pride.

Granny Brewster fell back in her chair with a hoot of laughter while Whitney continued to look befuddled. Annika, Thea, and Gordon jumped up and hurried outside after the boys. They all gathered quietly around the edge of the big washtub.

"Now be quiet, or you'll scare him," James warned.

Plunking down contentedly in the middle of the mud and twigs was a fat, sleepy-eyed frog.

"I don't believe it!" Annika whispered hoarsely. She'd gone all over creation looking for frogs, and here was one sitting in a tub of mud right outside her back door.

"We can sell this stuff and make a fortune!" James exclaimed. "We'll have plenty of money to buy Millie a new bicycle."

"Wait a minute," interrupted Thea. "You can't be serious. Who's going to buy mud?"

"It's *not* mud. It's dogwood stew," James corrected her. "And every kid in the village will want to buy some when they hear it's guaranteed to catch frogs."

"Guaranteed?" Thea said with a laugh. "You can't guarantee a thing like catching frogs. Can you, Daddy?"

Gordon shook his head. "I never heard of it."

"That's the biggest bunch of baloney I ever heard!" Annika finally burst out.

James looked at her with that air of superiority he seemed to have taken on about everything. "Well, you just wait and see for yourself, baloney head!"

"Who are you calling a baloney head?"

The contented fat frog who had become the object of a growing argument began to twitch nervously in the middle of his dogwood stew. Suddenly, he took a flying leap out of the tub and into the bushes.

"Our frog! Catch him!" yelled the boys.

Without thinking much about it, everybody jumped into the bushes at once. Granny and Whitney, who had just stepped outside, ran back in and emerged seconds later waving large wire strainers.

"We can't let him get away!" wailed James. "We won't be able to sell any dogwood stew!"

"Why not?" asked Annika, pawing through her mother's potted geraniums on the back porch steps.

"Nobody'll believe us if we caught a frog and then it got away."

"Y'all hush!" warned Granny. The frog had bounced out of the bushes and landed in the grass. She was carefully sneaking up on it with her wire strainer cocked menacingly over her shoulder. Everyone froze.

Suddenly, Heinz trotted around the corner. He gave one short, sharp yap at the frog and launched himself towards it.

"Grab Heinz!" everyone shouted.

Gordon tackled the dachshund, but now the big dogs had been alerted and came careening around the other side of the house. Soon everyone was chasing dogs instead of frogs. In the confusion, the frog disappeared altogether.

"Now we've lost him for good!" moaned James.

"Well, it's a test," responded Annika. "If this dogwood stew is guaranteed to catch frogs, that means you'll catch him again."

James still looked woeful.

"You can't sell a product you don't believe in," Thea said.

"That's right, Beeper," Gordon agreed. "One frog does not a fortune make."

"Dad, are you quoting Thoreau again?" Annika
wanted to know.

"No, that's pure Anderson. Thanks for the com-
pliment."

James was still struggling. Slowly, he began to
brighten. "Well, we'll catch another one, won't we,
guys?"

"Yes, of course. Of course!" One by one, everyone
agreed enthusiastically. After all, why not?

"Isn't it better to be optimistic, Dad?" James
asked.

"Absolutely."

"I'll bet he comes back," piped up Austin, who was
usually optimistic about most things. He folded his
arms smugly. "Don't worry, James. If he doesn't, we'll
just wait until we catch another one."

"Right," agreed Andrew who couldn't let his twin
have the last word. "And then everyone will *know* that
dogwood stew can catch frogs."

"Yeah," said James. He poked a long stick into the
washtub and gave the stew a stir, half hoping the frog
might pop up then and there. He still wasn't entirely
sure he hadn't lost his fortune.

Annika put her arm around James and tried to
comfort him. "Thanks for thinking of Millie, Beeper.
There's lots of other ways we can make money."

But James seemed set on proving to the world
that dogwood stew could catch frogs.

"Granny B., do you think it would be okay to pray
about this?" he asked her that night. It had been bug-
ging him all day. All through the morning's continued
search around the Pink Farm, during his peanut but-

ter and jelly sandwich at lunch, his afternoon bike ride, while helping Granny shuck the corn for supper, even through his ice cream and chocolate sauce, and while getting the dirt scraped off his elbows at bath time.

Annika was practicing her piano seriously for once. "One and two and three and four and—" She stopped when she heard James's question and turned around to smile at her squeaky-clean little brother with his hair combed back into a wet point at the back of his neck, just like a duck's tail.

"Pray about a frog?" she couldn't help asking with a laugh.

"Well, why not?" said Granny Brewster, pulling the little boy into her lap. "Don't you know the story about Peter the fisherman and how he went to fish, but there just wasn't any fish? Jesus came along and said, 'Peter, why don't y'all go fishin' and catch us some of those nice Galilee fish for our breakfast?' But Peter said, 'We can't catch any, sir,' 'cause he didn't know it was the Lord speakin' to him, you see. So Jesus said, 'Throw your nets over the other side of the boat.' Well, they did and do you know, they caught so many fish they couldn't get 'em all in the boat! Then they knew it was the Lord, 'cause it was a miracle, you see, and Peter was so excited, he jumped right out of the boat and swam to meet Him. I reckon if Jesus could bring 'em all that fish, He could bother with one little frog, don't you?"

"But things don't happen like that today, Granny B.," Annika said doubtfully.

"Well, how do you know they don't? You're just goin' around with your eyes shut, girl. There's mira-

cles everyday. It's a miracle that Millie Brown did
get herself killed, and it'll be another miracle if you
ever get her on a bicycle again."

"What if the frog doesn't come back, Granny B.?"
asked James. "Does that mean I didn't pray right?"

"No, it just means the frog wasn't meant to come
back. The Lord had somewhere else for him to go.
That's how you have to believe."

Annika swiveled back around to her piano and
slowly began playing again. It seemed an absurd thing
to pray about a frog. It began to bug her. All through
her piano practice. Even more than the wrong notes.
And all during her strawberry-scented bubble bath.
And all during her milk and brownies and bedtime
checkers game with her father. She was good at beat-
ing Gordon, but tonight she couldn't concentrate.

"Dad," she said after Granny had gone upstairs to
take her bath and James had gone to bed, "how come
that guy Thoreau went to live in the woods anyways?"

"Well, he wanted to get away from the conven-
tions of society and live as natural a life as he could.
Close to nature, that is."

"Do you think he cared much about frogs?"

"He cared about everything in nature. Why?"

"Well, do you think God cares about frogs?"

Gordon looked at her quizzically. "Why, I think He
does."

Annika propped her elbows on the table and
sighed. "James is praying that God will send him his
frog back. Don't you think that's a bit much?"

Gordon laughed. "Who knows? To James, it probably isn't."

oose Thoreau wouldn't have thought it
?"

snook his head. "Buzzie, what are you
say?"

Annika moved restlessly in her chair. "Well, if you don't think it's dumb and Thoreau doesn't think it's dumb and God doesn't think it's dumb, then I guess *I'm* dumb!"

"You don't believe anything will come of it, is that it?"

"Yeah," Annika admitted. "I don't. And James is going to be awfully disappointed."

Gordon collected two of her checkers in one move. Annika groaned. "There are lots of disappointments in life, Buzz," Gordon said mischievously. "Not getting what you want is one of them."

"Like winning at checkers, you garbanzo bean!"

"What? You think I should *let* you win? No way! You gotta learn to win. There's nothing like a well-earned victory."

"Oh, Daddy, you're being horrid."

"Sorry, sweetheart. We all have crises of faith. I don't know that Thoreau necessarily believed in anything except the heaven over and under his feet. And sometimes, to be quite honest, I haven't either. But I guess it's not important how your prayers get answered. It's learning how to pray that matters."

"Praying is more than wishing, isn't it, Daddy?" Annika asked as she surveyed the checkerboard.

Gordon thoughtfully contemplated his daughter. "Prayer is holy, Buzz. That I know. It's not a wishing well. Some of us take a long time to learn that."

Annika slowly moved a checker across the board, reluctant to let it go in case she'd made a mistake. Once your fingers let go of the checker, that was it. You couldn't take it back. She looked at her father for a sign, a smirk, a smile, uplifted eyebrows. He only gave her a nod.

"It's kind of like praying, isn't it?" he remarked. "A move into the unknown."

Annika smiled. "Oh, Daddy." And with a lift of her fingers, she let go.

James woke her up eagerly at first light, the way he did on Christmas morning.

"I'm going down to look for my frog. Come!" It was a simple command as well as an invitation.

Annika propped herself up on one elbow and looked at him with wonder for a moment. He had come back to her with a single word. "Come!"

Still in their pajamas, they sneaked carefully down the stairs as if the slightest creak might send their frog hopping. Sam Ting greeted them at the back door with an inquisitive sniff and an "uh-oh," causing them both to jump and bump into each other.

"Sshhh!" warned James. "Be—very—quiet!"

They stepped outside into the misty morning as if stepping out into another world. The shadows of the pines and the garden and the cows moving in the meadow appeared to be unfinished sculptures still in the process of being created. The grass was fresh and wet underneath their bare feet, and they could see the single drops of dew clinging like pearls to the trailing vine across the house and the spider's web under the porch rail.

The outer world was dim and still a mystery, but everything that was close around them quivered with the delicate wonder of new life. Annika trembled with the excitement of sudden expectation.

Birds were beginning to twitter around the farm, and they could hear Prince's snorts and movements inside the barn. The rest of the world slept on. Then something else broke the silence, something low and intermittent and of the earth, like a cricket's chirp, only heavier and more subdued.

They came to the edge of the washtub and peeked in. James reached over and tightly gripped his sister's hand. He wanted to screech and yell the way he had the other day. But instead he stood perfectly still and stared, barely breathing at the answer to his prayer, croaking away as joyfully as if it were the first day of Creation.

Dogwood Stew and Catnip Tea

DOGWOOD STEW
OPTIMISTICALLY GUARANTEED TO CATCH FROGS!!
$1.00 A JAR OR 25¢ IF YOU BRING YOUR OWN.
ALL PROCEEDS GO TO THE
MILLIE BROWN BICYCLE ACCIDENT FUND.
HELP MILLIE! CATCH A FROG!

Annika stood back and looked at her sign with smug satisfaction. Gordon and Grover had built them a little stall at the entrance to the Pink Farm, and sitting on top of it was the frog, contentedly encased in an old fish aquarium loaded up with dogwood stew. They had collected old jars from all over the neighborhood and an extra couple of washtubs, so that there was enough dogwood stew to catch an army of frogs.

"Tilt the sign just a little to the right, Daddy," Annika instructed. "There."

Gordon deftly nailed the sign to the front of the stall. Now they were ready for business.

"Okay, Andrew and Austin, go round up some customers!" Annika ordered. She had made identical signs and tied them with a bunch of green balloons to the backs of their bicycles. They were supposed to ride around the village and attract as much attention as possible. To make sure they did, Annika decided to dress them up like frogs. She mixed green food coloring into a jar of Thea's theatrical makeup and rubbed it all over their faces, hands, legs, and in their hair. They each wore identical green sweatshirts and shorts and a pair of green diving flippers on their feet.

"Now, it's your turn, Beeps," she said.

James took one look at the twins and ran and hid under the porch. "No way!" he screamed, convulsed with laughter.

"Come on, Beeper!" yelled Andrew. "You've got to look like a frog, too!"

"Yeah, Beeper!" echoed Austin.

"Forget it!"

"Beeper, don't be a spoilsport," pleaded Annika.

"Are *you* going to paint *your* face green?" James challenged her from under the porch.

"Well, no, I mean—"

"I'll do it if you do!"

"But I'm in charge!"

"That shouldn't make any difference."

"Yeah, it wouldn't be fair, Annika," chorused the twins.

"All right," Annika agreed. "You guys just better sell this stuff!"

Their first customer was a man out walking his
dog. He seemed to be deep in thought when he suddenly saw two green faces smiling at him.

"Is it Halloween?" he said, stopping to read their
sign. "What on earth is dogwood stew?"

"It's for a frog's wedding," Annika said, smiling
greenly up at him.

"A frog's wedding?" The man laughed. "Who's
Millie Brown?"

"A girl who got hit by a car on her bicycle. We're
trying to buy her a new bike so she won't be afraid to
ride again."

The man laughed some more. "You kids deserve
a medal. Here." He pulled out a five-dollar bill.

"Wow!" exclaimed James. "That's five jars!"

"No, no, you can keep the stew! I haven't been
invited to any frog weddings."

Granny came sauntering down the driveway.
"How're y'all doin'?" she called. "Got yourself a customer already?"

"We made five dollars, Granny!" James exclaimed
proudly.

"I think we sold lemonade in my day," said the
man. "This is something new."

"Well, we've got lemonade up at the house,"
Granny offered.

"Oh, thanks, but no thanks. I just stopped to find
out what dogwood stew was."

Granny laughed. "It's just an old family recipe."

"Well, good luck. I hope you sell lots of it!"

"Thanks, mister," said James.

"Why don't y'all sell something to drink as well?"

Granny suggested. "Not everybody's gonna want a jar of dogwood stew."

"We should sell catnip tea," Annika said. "What *is* catnip tea anyways?"

"I don't think you'd sell much of that either," said Granny. "In the summer folks would rather have a nice, cool glass of lemonade or iced tea."

"There's a big pitcher of iced tea in the fridge," Annika thought out loud. "We could pretend it was catnip tea. Couldn't we, Granny?"

"Well—"

"Oh, Granny B., you're brilliant! What a great idea!"

Granny lifted her eyebrows. "I suppose you want me to bring it down here in a jug, is that it?"

"Oh, Granny, you wouldn't mind, would you?"

"Well, you're not paintin' me up like no frog, I can tell you that."

The day was a bigger success than they'd ever imagined. Soon the yard was full of little boys and bicycles and curious villagers. Word spread as quickly around town as news of Millie's bicycle accident. People who had never given the Browns more than a snide remark were suddenly touched enough to come and contribute something. Even if they didn't take any dogwood stew with them, they were glad to sample some of Granny's homemade "catnip" iced tea.

The more people came, the more Annika's family thought up things to do. Thea offered rides on Prince for a nickel while Whitney set herself up as a quick sketch artist. Grover put on a magic show, of course, and went around pulling pennies out of kids' ears.

Soon he had them pulling nickels and dimes out of their pockets.

"Forty-two dollars and twenty-five cents." Annika counted it all up slowly. "Will that be enough to buy Millie a bike, Dad?"

"A good used one, sure."

"I wish Millie could have been here today," she mused happily.

They were all sitting on the porch and feeling proud of themselves. The Mowatt twins had gone home to wash off their green faces, and Annika was ready to do the same. She looked down at the box of money in her lap and gave a happy sigh. For once it seemed the Great Annika Josephine Anderson Plan was working.

Almost.

An hour later the doorbell rang shrilly.

"I bet I know who that is!" Thea yelled up the stairs.

"It's *not* funny!" Annika shouted down from the bathroom.

"Somebody answer the door!" Whitney called from the kitchen.

"Not me!" said Thea, ducking out of sight.

"Well, I guess that leaves old Dad." Gordon reluctantly got up from his chair.

"*Mister* Anderson!" shrieked Mrs. Mowatt the minute he opened the door. "Will you look?"

Gordon looked. The twins stood crying in front of her, their skin and hair the color of cheese mold.

"I have scrubbed these boys with everything I can

think of, and they're still green! What did your daughter do to them?"

"Food coloring," Gordon explained. "Totally harmless."

"Totally harmless?!"

"I'm sure it'll wear off by the time their high school prom rolls around."

"Oh, really? Meanwhile, my sons will look like Martians for the next ten years?" The twins cried even harder.

"Well, maybe they can start a Martian club with Annika and James."

"It's *not* funny, Gordon! What am I supposed to do?"

James came solemnly down the stairs. He looked like he was about to throw up any minute. "Hi, guys," he said forlornly. "I'm green, too."

Andrew and Austin took one look at him and, forgetting their own greenness, burst out laughing.

James began to giggle. "What are you laughing at me for?"

"Please. Come in," Gordon said amiably to Mrs. Mowatt. "We'll make some green tea or something."

As they sat down in the living room, Annika slowly descended the stairs. An hour in the bathtub had done nothing but turn the bathtub green as well. Her whole plan had turned into a total disaster. She'd really have to go live in the woods now. At least, she'd be camouflaged there.

"I'm terribly, awfully sorry, Mrs. Mowatt," she said miserably. "It's all my fault and responsibility."

"Look at Annika!" little Austin yelled out. "She looks like Frankenstein!"

The boys and even Mrs. Mowatt suddenly began to laugh harder than they'd cried. Somehow Annika looked the worst of all of them. She threw her green hands up in the air and walked back out of the room.

"Oh, great! I look like Frankenstein! Thanks a lot, guys."

"Now Annika has green gloves," teased James. "Granny Green-Gloves Annika!"

"Granny Green-Gloves Annika Frankenstein!" shouted Austin.

She was Frankenstein for a week. All the kids in the neighborhood came to see her, and when they got a glimpse, they ran away screaming. It greatly irritated her at first, but then, deciding to make the most of it, she went charging after them with her eyes half-closed, her legs stiff and mechanical, and her arms waving wildly in front of her.

After a week, playing Frankenstein wore off as well as the food coloring. But the kids still screamed and ran whenever they went past the Pink Farm. Wherever she went, one look was enough to start them screaming all over again.

"I've never heard so much hollerin' and carryin' on in all my born days!" exclaimed Granny as one more shriek split the air.

"You're tellin' me!" said Annika. She was fuming. "I'm Frankenstein for life!"

"Maybe we should sell tickets," suggested Thea. "People are always willing to pay for a thrill."

"Why don't you go paint your face green?"

"Annika, you never ask anybody how to do things. You just go ahead and do them and get yourself into trouble."

"Well, I still don't deserve to be the neighborhood Frankenstein. I can't go anywhere now without some stupid kid screaming at me. I'm getting just a wee bit tired of it!"

"Well, now you know how Millie Brown feels," Granny said, picking up her crochet hook from where she'd dropped it on the floor.

Annika was about to bite into a peach. She looked at Granny. "I guess maybe you're right. I never thought—"

"Never thought what it must be like to be Millie Brown?" finished Granny.

"Kids don't scream at her."

"But they run away from her."

"When's she getting out of the hospital?" Thea asked.

"I think next week."

"Have you picked out a bicycle for her yet?"

"Yes, a nice, red shiny one from Gary's Bike Shop. It was fifty dollars used, but he said we could have it for forty-two. He's real nice."

"So when you reckon on giving it to her?" asked Granny.

Annika rolled the fuzzy ripe peach around in her hands. "I don't know. Depends on how she is."

"Hey, Franky! Yoo-hoo, Frankeee!"

"The little weirdos—I'm going to give them all a knuckle sandwich if they don't stop!"

"Just ignore them," said Thea with a yawn. "They'll outgrow it."

"Yeah, in twenty years, maybe?"

Annika went to the window and stared out. One of the kids saw her and, pointing, let out a bloodcurdling shriek that sent Granny's crochet hook flying across the room again.

Annika marched out onto the porch and firmly dug her fists into her hips. "STOP IT, RIGHT NOW!" she yelled at them.

Suddenly, Gordon appeared at the gate. If there was one thing Annika was glad for in her father, it was his size. Nobody dared run away from Gordon Anderson. The kids slowly wheeled their bikes back in response to his command.

Annika couldn't hear what he was saying to them. But she felt a tremendous sense of relief. She thought again of Millie and all the times she'd been treated badly with no decent father to speak up for her. There'd been nobody to speak up for her.

Some things wore off, like paint. But other things never did.

Queen
of the Bicycles

Annika stretched herself out on the grass in front of a long roll of paper and began to paint in bright, large letters: "WELCOME HOME, MILLIE."

"I want this sign to be big as a house," she told James who was peering over her shoulder.

"Big as a house?" James said with lifted eyebrows.

"Wouldn't it be great if we could tie it to an airplane and fly it right over her house?" Annika was feeling inspired.

"But we don't know anybody who has an airplane," James pointed out.

"Oh, James," sighed Annika. "Why do you always have to be so practical?"

"Well, how are you going to fly this sign over Millie's house without an airplane?"

"We're not, Beep. Forget it. We'll just make a really, really *big* sign."

"Are we really going to have a parade?" James wanted to know, hopping from foot to foot.

"Of course. It's going to be the best and biggest parade this village has ever seen."

"Can I lead it?"

"Sure."

"Can Barney be in it, and Heinz and Red and Toby and Sammie and—"

"It's a parade, Beeper, not a circus!"

"Are we going to be frogs again?"

"Only you, Beeper!"

And, whooping and hollering, she chased him with her paintbrush all around the yard.

Annika made the sign long enough to hang between the old iron bedstead and the Browns' rusty signpost on the opposite side of the dirt road. On the day Millie was supposed to come home, she and James rounded up all the kids in the neighborhood who would come, and because it was going to be a parade, that was most of them.

James was the leader, wearing his fireman's hat and with Barney on his shoulder in a ruffled collar. Annika followed, riding Millie's new bike which she'd carefully decorated with streamers of crepe paper ribbon, balloons, and a sign on the back spelling "Millie" in glittery gold letters. Lining up behind her was a long procession of bicycles gleaming in the sun, and at the end, Thea on her horse. She'd braided Prince's mane and tail and wore her own hair in a long French braid. The two of them looked very beautiful together, Annika thought with a sigh.

Red and Toby raced around in circles, barking with excitement.

"Can't they come?" James begged.

"No, sorry, Beeper," Annika said firmly. "They'll just stir things up. We can't let them go running around the Browns' place. You saw that beast hiding under their porch. Who knows what would happen? Red and Toby would go berserk!"

Annika didn't even like the idea of Barney riding along. But James insisted he wouldn't freak, and besides, he wasn't going without him.

"Y'all look great!" called Granny from the porch.

Whitney was running around taking pictures while Gordon backed the station wagon slowly down the drive. It too had balloons flying from the antenna and tied to all the door handles.

Annika had told Millie's mother about the parade ahead of time, mostly to warn Mr. Brown, but Mrs. Brown was so excited she forgot it was supposed to be a surprise and told Millie all about it. When Millie and her mother finally came rattling down the road in their old pickup, Millie was reaching over and tootling the horn nonstop.

"Well, here they come!" Annika announced, feeling excited and nervous all at once. "Everybody in their places!"

"We'll be following behind," said Gordon with a wave. "Just go slowly and take your time."

"We will, Daddy," Annika said, climbing onto the red, shiny bicycle. It all seemed so strange suddenly. This parade, this bicycle, this day. It was, Annika thought, like the first day of a whole new life in a whole new world.

Millie hung her big head out the window, her face in a rapture of amazement. All the kids tooted their bike horns and yelled and waved back. She was suddenly surrounded by bicycles and streamers and balloons as well as a beautiful girl on a horse, and she took on the role of Queen of the Bicycles as simply as if she'd been born to it.

They rattled and honked, cheered and waved their way down the hill, past the corner where Millie's accident had occurred, and onto the dirt road that led to the end of the village. Millie waved both arms out of the window, holding her fingers up in a V sign, and at times she laughed in a hoarse voice and banged exuberantly on the door of the truck.

"Hooray! Hooray!" she yelled back at all her fans. Everyone not in the parade had come out to the road to watch the procession and waved cheerfully back at her. It had turned out to be a glorious day, the sort of day when the sky and water sparkled in unison, and the birds swooped and cheer-cheered, and the fish and porpoises danced in the air above the Sound. It was a day meant for a parade, a day meant for Millie.

At last they reached the end of the road where the welcome banner hung, and Millie's greatest moment seemed to come as the old truck broke through the sign the way a runner breaks through the finish line.

"Hooray for Millie! Hooray for Millie!" she shouted out the window, her arms upraised in triumph. She'd done it. She'd made it. And everyone cheered in response.

"Hooray for Millie! Hooray for Millie!"

It didn't occur to her or anyone else that she'd come back to exactly what she'd left—that there wasn't any change there, or any cheer in it either. Only the frenzied barking of dogs among a rotting garbage heap and a crazy old man waving a shotgun.

"What's goin' on here!" he demanded from the front door. "Git these kids off my property!"

"Oh, shut up, you old nincompoop!" Mrs. Brown yelled at him, slamming the truck door. "I told you, it's on account of Millie's comin' home. Now go on inside and quit makin' a fool of yourself."

Mr. Brown muttered something. Then making a threatening jab with his gun, he slowly retreated back into the house.

It was enough to dispel the mood of the day though, and the kids began to fidget nervously on their bikes, eager to clear out of there. The Andersons hurried forward to help Mrs. Brown get Millie out of the truck.

She was still in her cast and on crutches. But she seemed out of pain and only perplexed by the whole awkward weight of her leg. She limped slowly forward.

"Hi, Millie," Annika said quickly. She wanted out of there, too. Millie wouldn't look at her, but stared off in the distance.

"Millie, I hope you'll believe me this time. I really am very sorry, and I do wish you'd let me be your friend again. All of us want to be better friends to you. We even bought you a present to prove it. Look."

She stood back from the red bicycle sparkling

with glitter and balloons. With her heart pounding, she watched for Millie's reaction.

"We believe in you, Millie," she heard herself saying, afraid suddenly Millie wouldn't understand. "When your leg gets better, you're going to be able to ride better than ever. Better than anyone! Because this is a *great* bike, Millie. And we want you to have it."

Millie looked at it curiously. "For me?" she said, wrinkling up her nose.

"For you, Millie."

Millie looked at her mother. "Can I keep it, Ma?"

"Well, I don't know—" Mrs. Brown said with a nervous twitter to her voice. She hadn't been told about the bicycle. "I don't want you gettin' in any more accidents."

Annika gulped. "Mrs. Brown, I promise to help Millie. I mean, I'll try to make sure it won't happen again. We just thought it would help her confidence if she could ride a bike again."

"Well, it won't do her no good with a cast on her leg," reasoned Mrs. Brown who had a hard time seeing anything but the obvious.

"It'll give her something to look forward to," Annika tried to explain. "When her cast comes off."

Millie still wouldn't look at Annika. She looked only at the bike. She stared at it as if nothing else existed in the world. A strange expression came over her face, one of wonder and confusion and hope. Desperately trying to struggle out of all that was locked inside of her, she saw the bike not as a threat, but as some sort of magical, glittering bird come to set her free.

"Can I keep the balloons, too?" she asked, squinting her eyes against the sun. Then for a moment she looked at Annika.

"Sure!" said Annika. "Are we friends again, Millie?" She stuck out her hand.

"Yeah," Millie said sheepishly. She reached out and grasped Annika's hand tightly.

"Hooray!" Annika cheered. Her own heart was flying free, too.

A Piece
of Corn Bread

There were three phases of Whitney Brewster Anderson's work:

1. Door partly open.
2. Door closed but unlocked.
3. Door closed, locked, and bolted.

She had been in the third phase for the last couple of weeks. No one had a clue what she was doing or why. Only James and Millie Brown had been allowed in there. Annika had visions of pink and golden winged babies floating around like giant butterflies with James and Millie chasing after them. How Millie could chase flying babies in her cast, she wasn't sure. But it was useless trying to get a word out of either one of them.

On the day Whitney unlocked the door to her studio, she invited Millie and Mrs. Brown for tea.

"Are you finally going to let us see it?" Annika demanded.

"I thought so," Whitney answered her with an exultant ring to her voice.

Annika regarded her mother with a mystified stare. "Aren't you going to give us the teeniest, weeniest *hint* first?"

Whitney beamed triumphantly. "Nope."

"Oh, Mom, the suspense is killing us!"

"Go help Granny with the cake. That will get your mind off it."

Annika wandered into the kitchen where James was carefully cracking an egg into a large bowl. Granny Brewster hovered over him like a hawk.

"Don't get any shell in there, or you'll have a time gettin' it out," she cautioned.

James looked up as Annika walked in. "Hi, Annika. Granny B. and me are making a carrot cake."

"Granny and I," corrected Granny.

"Oh, yum! Can I help?" Annika asked.

"Sure," Granny Brewster said with excitement. "How about gratin' the carrots?"

Annika began searching through the junk drawer for a carrot peeler. "Mom sure is making a big fuss about her new sculpture."

"I can't wait to see it," said Granny, turning on the mixer. "Now, James, don't stick your fingers in there."

"I can't wait either," said James, thinking more of the cake than his mother's latest artistic creation.

"What do you mean, *you* can't wait? You saw her in there!" Annika appealed. "What was she doing?"

James shrugged. "I dunno. Just drawing."

"Drawing what? You can tell us now, Beeper."

"No, you'll just have to find out for yourself."

"Well, we'll find out this afternoon, won't we?" said Granny. "Whatever it is, I'm sure we won't know what it is anyways."

"Do you think Mrs. Brown will let Millie go to that school?" Annika asked, changing the subject. It was one of the reasons Whitney had asked Mrs. Brown for tea.

"Well, it's certainly what Millie needs. I think your father'll talk Mrs. Brown into it. This accident was a big scare for her. I think she'll let Millie go now."

"I hope so," Annika said. "I sure hope so."

Granny Brewster insisted everyone dress up for the tea. "Wouldn't it be fun if for once everyone looked like civilized human beings that hadn't just rolled out of bed?"

"No, it wouldn't be fun," argued James.

Whitney's version of dressing up was wearing a long white caftan and dangling black jeweled earrings. Gordon wore a bow tie. James combed his hair and finally consented to wearing a striped dress shirt with his usual baggy shorts. Thea had a new rainbow-colored skirt that swished and glistened when she walked, and Annika couldn't decide what to wear. She finally settled on a pink and purple striped sun dress, a bright pink headband studded with rhinestones, and a pair of Thea's pink feather earrings. She thought none of them had ever looked so elegant.

They were preparing the tea things when James burst through the kitchen door.

"I *found* it!" he announced, looking at Annika with wide-eyed excitement.

"Found what?" everyone chorused.

James came over and tugged on Annika's arm. "Do I still get my ice cream and root beer and elephant ride?" he wanted to know.

Annika quickly pushed James out the door before he could blurt out anything else.

"You found it? You mean—"

"Yeah! You said if I found it you'd—"

"Where, Beeper?" Annika said impatiently. She'd practically given up on it.

A guilty smile stole quietly across James's face. "You *promise* now?"

"James Anderson! Did *you* take it?"

"No! No!" he protested, giggling. "But I know who did!"

"Who?!"

"Mrs. Brown!"

"*Mrs. Brown?*"

She tore after him around the side of the house and came to an abrupt halt. There coming grandly up the walk in a flurry of dachshund and golden retrievers was Mrs. Brown. A flaming red satin hat was skewered to the top of her head like a tomato wedge on a shish kebab. A single white silk rose bobbed up and down on top of it with every step she took. Annika stared at her in horror.

"Why, hello, Mrs. Brown! Hello, Millie!" Whitney greeted them gaily from the porch.

"Hello there!" Granny called out next. Annika gave her a panicked glance. Granny's eyes were bulging even larger so that they filled up her entire glasses. Her eyebrows were raised almost to her hairline. She felt her dentures coming loose, and with a sharp cough, she turned quickly to readjust them as well as her self-composure.

Then, with a bright smile, she turned back around and said, "My, what a bee-yoo-ti-ful hat, Mrs. Brown!"

Mrs. Brown glowed with pride. "Millie gave it to me for my birthday yesterday. I've always wanted a fancy red hat."

Millie, now cast-free, smiled around at nobody in particular, greatly pleased with herself.

"And where does she suppose Millie got it from?" Annika whispered, fiercely pulling James back around the house. "I suppose the thought never entered her brain. What on earth am I going to do now?"

"Beats me," shrugged James. "Do I still get my root beer and—"

"Oh, hush, Beeper! Can't you see, I'm in big trouble now? Granny's best hat!"

"James? Annika? Where are you?" Whitney called out the back door. "They're here. We're about to have tea."

"Well, here goes." Annika gulped. "This may be the end of me, Beeper. It's been nice knowing you."

It was the best carrot cake in the world, but Annika couldn't eat more than two bites of it. She avoided looking at anybody, certain they'd all know she was behind this thing on Mrs. Brown's head. One suspicious "Oh, Annika" look and she'd throw up. She continued to miserably twiddle her fork around her plate.

Mrs. Brown and Millie ate more cake than anybody and were enjoying themselves immensely. Finally, Gordon brought up the subject of the school.

"But Millie's already been to school. They won't take her no more," said Mrs. Brown, picking up cake crumbs with her fingers and licking them off one at a time.

"Well, it's not a school exactly," explained Gordon. "She could live there and have lots of friends her own age. She'd be taught how to make things for craft stores. Just think, Millie would have a fun job and lots of nice friends. She'd be happy. Do you think Millie's happy now, Mrs. Brown?"

Millie was interested. "Can I go, Ma? I'll make friends," she said through a mouthful of cake.

Mrs. Brown suddenly began to cry. The once magnificent red hat slipped further across the back of her head. The white rose was as wilted and wrinkled looking as her face.

"I don't want Millie to go," she sniffed into a dirty handkerchief.

Millie reached out and stroked her mother's arm. "It's all right, sweetie. It's all right, precious," she cooed.

Whitney rose to her feet, looking perfectly angelic in her long, white robe. "Look, please think about it, Mrs. Brown. Think of Millie and what's best for her. Right now, I want you all to come see something."

"Ah! The moment we've all been waiting for!" Gordon exclaimed. He took his wife's arm, and the procession to the Pink Studio began.

"Where do you suppose Millie found that outlandish hat?" Thea whispered to Annika.

Annika's heart jumped. "You don't want to know."

Whitney opened the studio door and led them all

inside. Her face glowing with pride, she nodded towards a near-life-size plaster model perched on a pedestal in the center of the room.

She looked at them all expectantly. "Well, what do you think?"

Posed slightly above them, four very realistic children had been caught in suspended motion. A black child turned the page of a book; a fair-skinned boy, strongly resembling James, crouched behind a frog; a little Oriental girl precariously balanced a tower of blocks; and the fourth child, her leg in a cast, leaned forward on a pair of crutches, and with a wide open mouth, laughed at them all.

"Why, that's Millie!" gasped Thea.

"And me!" cried James.

"Who're the other two?" wondered Annika.

"It's called 'All Are Precious,'" Whitney said in a hushed voice. "Do you all like it?"

"Like it? Darling, it's magnificent!" Gordon said with sincere praise.

"It's the best thing you've ever done, Mom," said Thea.

Granny Brewster simply shook her head, her eyes brimming with tears. "Well, sugah, I always knew you had it in you somewheres. I'm glad to see it's finally come out."

Whitney continued to glow, numb with pleasure. "Do you all really think so? Really and truly?"

Annika smiled up at her mother with a quiet pride. "It sure beats all those flying babies, Mom."

Mrs. Brown stood apart, murmuring with amazement while Millie limped gingerly up to it and, reaching out a finger, shyly touched the replica of her own face.

"Is that me?" she asked, her nose wrinkling in wonder.

"Yes, Millie," Whitney responded eagerly, "and all the other children in the world who are handicapped. You're their representative, an ambassador for all those who are still unborn."

Millie was confused. "What's 'ambassador'?"

"A friend, Millie."

"Is that really Millie?" asked Mrs. Brown.

"Millie was my model, Mrs. Brown, along with James. I'm going to give this to the Teen Pregnancy Center. They asked me to do a sculpture for them."

"Teen Pregnancy Center? What's that?" Mrs. Brown looked shocked.

"It's a counseling center for unwed mothers. I hope this sculpture might make them think a little about letting their babies live rather than destroying them."

"I don't know what Millie's got to do with it."

"I think Millie is just as special as other children, Mrs. Brown. I think we've all come to think that. She has many unique gifts all her own. She was my inspiration, you see, for this sculpture. That's why it would be so good for her to go to this new school. So she can learn how to use her gifts and be an inspiration to lots of other people as well."

"Well, I'll think about it," Mrs. Brown said with a slight pout. "But I don't think Millie should be going to any Teen Pregnancy Center."

"No, no, Millie won't be going there," Whitney

emphasized. "Just the *sculpture*. It'll be in a pretty garden, with a fountain. That's all right, isn't it?"

"I guess so. Just as long as people don't think it's Millie who's pregnant."

Whitney looked at her horrified. "Oh, no, Mrs. Brown! You completely misunderstand!" She looked helplessly at Gordon who winked at her and was about to say something when Granny firmly took hold of the confused Mrs. Brown's arm and marched her towards the door.

"Mrs. Brown, I bet you'd like to take a piece of cake home to Mr. Brown," she said sweetly.

"Oh, don't bother. He ain't used to cake," said Mrs. Brown, glum at the mention of her husband.

"Well, come to the kitchen and I'll pack up some for you and Millie then."

"Well, all right." And as she left on Granny's arm and in Granny's hat, she whispered loudly in Granny's ear, "Don't you think that was a pretty statue of Millie? I don't know why she had to leave her cast on though."

"Why, it'll make Millie famous," Granny replied.

"Famous?"

"Yeah, and when she goes to this school and learns to make things, everybody'll want to buy them."

"No kiddin'?"

When Mrs. Brown and Millie finally left, Whitney collapsed at the kitchen table and, with her head between her hands, burst into tears.

"It's the best thing I've ever done!" she cried with overflowing emotion.

"Yes, it is," soothed Gordon, handing her a box of tissues.

"Poor Mrs. Brown—she just didn't understand!" And Whitney began to laugh as well as cry. "Oh, Gordon, it's pathetic. Really! And that hat! It looked like one of those monstrosities my mother used to wear."

Everyone was gathered around Whitney except, for once, Granny Brewster. She had simply disappeared. Swallowing the hard lump of guilt that remained in her throat, Annika quietly left her mother to her emotions and sauntered up the stairs.

Granny was sitting in the rocking chair facing the open window. There was a small book in her lap.

It was a few moments before Annika could bring herself to say, "Hey, Granny B."

Granny turned around and closed her book. "Well, your mamma's done good, hasn't she?"

Annika nodded. For the first time, she realized how greatly she admired her mother. "Do you think she'll be famous someday?"

"I've—no doubt about it."

Annika wanted to blurt out everything that was on her heart, but somehow it wouldn't come. It was all stuck down in her stomach somewhere. She stood there transfixed, staring down at her pink plastic shoes.

"Well, I reckon you'll be starting school real soon," Granny said, the rocker creaking gently under her weight.

School? Annika hadn't given it a thought. The summer promised to go on forever. She didn't want to go back to school. Not yet anyway.

"School? Yuck!" she groaned.

"Oh, you'll be glad to go back. We've all got to keep goin' in life, you know. Nothin' can stay the same forever. I reckon it's time for me to be goin' as well."

"What? On account of me, Granny B.? Oh, please don't! Oh, Granny B., if you only knew how sorry, how wicked I feel! I never meant to give your hat away! Honest! It all seems like the worst joke ever, but it wasn't! I knew Millie had taken it, but she wouldn't give it back. That's when she had her accident. I was so angry with her for lying to me."

Annika rushed in and sobbed out the whole story into her grandmother's lap. "Please forgive me, Granny B. It was the meanest thing I ever could have done. But I didn't mean it to be mean. I—I just thought it was the prettiest, I mean, I felt so pretty. Do you know what I mean?"

"That hat cost me fifty dollars," Granny reminisced slowly. "That was the earth in those days. I never wanted a hat so bad. I spent all of my savings on it, in fact. I wore it to your Uncle Grady's confirmation, and as I sat down, feelin' so proud and grand, there not two pews in front of me was Mrs. Tyler in the *same identical* hat! I was just mortified! I couldn't *stand* Mrs. Tyler. I thought she was the uppitiest, snootiest woman in the entire church, and there I had to sit and look at her wearing *my* hat all during your Uncle Grady's confirmation. I'd made him practice his piece for weeks. It was so good—he wrote it himself, you know—and I didn't hear a word of it. All I could think of was how I was going to escape Mrs. Tyler afterwards. It was a mighty blow to my pride. The Lord has

His ways of teaching us humility, but I never thought
He'd teach it to me twice with the same hat!"

Annika looked up tear-stained into her grandmother's face. "You're not mad at me then, Granny B.?"

"Good heavens, no!" Granny Brewster leaned
back her head and suddenly roared with laughter. "Oh,
I thought I'd die. I just thought I'd *die* when I saw her
comin' up the walk. I didn't think it was *my* hat, you
see. I thought, well, it was Mrs. Tyler all over again.
HA! HA! HA! The joke's on me again! HA! HA!"

Annika couldn't help joining in. Laughter spilled
out of her like a trumpet. "You mean it, Granny B.? You
really mean it?"

"Oh, child, you're goin' to be the end of me yet!
Honest, no child has ever given me as much joy as you.
And I mean that."

"But I've been a brat. A *real* brat to you, Granny
B."

"I don't deny that. Here. I want you to have this."
She gave Annika the little book she'd been holding in
her lap. "It's my diary from the summer. I've been
keeping track of all the splendid things I've seen from
this window. I wrote them down just for you so you
wouldn't miss anything. You should have seen the sea
lions floating by on a logjam. It was like the circus
come to town!"

"But I did see them, Granny! When I was in the
woods down by the water."

"Well, it's time you got your window back, Annika.
You don't need to run away to the woods anymore."

"But I don't want to run away, not from you or
Millie or anybody. I want to stay right here on the Pink

Farm with you and Mom and Dad and James and Thea forever and ever. That's all I want."

"Well, nothing can be forever, Annika. Someday you'll find the right thing to be and you'll go on. As will James and Thea. Livin' your life means you can't stay the same. If you love people, and let them love you, then you'll see what I mean."

"Oh, Granny B., why can't we all stay the same?" Annika said desperately. "Aren't you happy here?"

Granny chuckled. "I've never been happier."

"Then why do you want to go?"

There was a heavy sigh. "It's best to leave when the goin's good, I guess. With school startin', you'll need more space and less of me. This is your room, Annika. I've just been a guest. It's not where I belong."

"But—but—it *is* your room!" Annika realized in a breath that her jealousy and resentment were gone. She'd somehow opened her "inside room," just as her father had said.

"No, darlin', I know you mean it. But there's still a twinge in you that needs your old room back. It's as it should be."

"But, Granny B., you don't want to go back to Tennessee! Do you? We all love you so!" And Annika knew for the first time it was true.

Granny Brewster looked at her with a twinkle in her eye. "Tennessee? Who said I was goin' back there? No, I like it here. I'm goin' to buy me a little house and set up shop."

She poked at her thick, cotton candy cone of hair. "They need a good hairdresser around here."

*   *   *

A cold, stiff breeze whipped around the Queen Anne's lace on the hill of the Pink Farm. It was a reminder that things would be changing soon.

Annika sped down the driveway on her bicycle, feeling the exhilarating sting of autumn on her cheek all the way to Bedstead Corner where she met Millie for their daily bike ride. Millie was waiting. A couple of deflated balloons hung limply from the handlebars of her red bike, and a few, straggly streamers trailed from the spokes of the wheels. Her face shone with excitement.

"ANN'KA!" she cried the minute she saw her friend. "ANN'KA! GUESS WHAT?"

"WHAT?"

Millie surged forward on her bicycle, pedaling as fast as she could.

"What's up, Millie?" Annika demanded, braking alongside the road.

Millie couldn't speak at first. She hid her face in her hands and peeked playfully at Annika between her fingers.

"Come on, Millie! The suspense is killing me!"

"Guess!"

"Guess? Oh, Millie! Is it something new?"

Millie vigorously shook her head.

"I don't know. You won a million dollars."

"No!" Millie guffawed. She dropped her fingers and, making fists, raised them up in the air.

"I'm going to school!"

"Oh, Millie, that's terrific!"

"I can take my bike," Millie said proudly. "I can ride real good now, huh, Ann'ka?"

"You sure can, Millie."

"Watch, Ann'ka. Watch me."

"I'm watching."

Millie wheeled her bike around and, still somewhat unsteady, weaved her way determinedly up and down the side of the road. A crooked little sign spelling "Millie" in faded gold letters flapped behind her like a flimsy white flag.

Annika applauded her with gusto. In a strange way, she knew she would miss Millie.

Reaching down, she plucked up a handful of lace growing alongside the road. She'd press some into her diary when she got home. Then summer would be over, and she and James would pick apples instead.